CAN THE ELECT BE DECEIVED

Nanci C. Nixon

Copyright © 2021 Nanci C. Nixon

All rights reserved. No part of this publication may be reproduced, distributed, or transmitted in any form or by any means, including photocopying, recording, or other electronic or mechanical methods, without the prior written permission of the publisher, except in the case of brief quotations embodied in critical reviews and certain other noncommercial uses permitted by copyright law. For permission requests, write to the publisher, addressed "Attention: Book Rights and Permission," at the address below.

Published in the United States of America

ISBN 978-1-953904-95-9 (SC)
ISBN: 978-1-955243-01-8 (Ebook)

Nanci C. Nixon
Email: nancinixx@aol.com
Website: www.joiwooministries.net

Order Information and Rights Permission:
Quantity sales. Special discounts might be available on quantity purchases by corporations, associations, and others. For details, contact the publisher at the address above.

For Book Rights Adaptation and other Rights Permission. Call us at toll-free 1-888-945-8513 or send us an email at admin@stellarliterary.com.

"Now the Spirit expressly says that in latter times some will depart from the faith, giving heed to deceiving spirits and doctrines of demons, speaking lies in hypocrisy, having their own conscience seared with a hot iron..."

I Timothy 4:1-2, (NKJV)

"For false christs and false prophets will rise and show great signs and wonders to deceive if possible, even the elect."

Matthew 24: 24, (NKJV)

Dedicated to:

My mother... Hollen Ruth Nixon, aka...Kandy Kane; a precious invaluable gem, and the most influential woman in my life. You were nurturer, teacher, example, confidant, admonisher, and my friend. Most of all, there was never a time in my life when I needed you, and you were not there. Your presence with the Lord is most comforting, but your absence here on earth has been a major adjustment for me. I miss you desperately.

My precious children, Deirdre and Derek. You are the crème de la crème, and I could not ask for any greater blessing than you two. Your unconditional love and your unwavering support has meant the world to me. You've been awesome! I love you so much, and I am forever grateful to God for you.

Acknowledgments

- I am forever indebted to Apostle Frederick K.C. Price and Dr. Betty Price, whose Christ-like earthly examples of impeccable character and unwavering integrity showed me how to live a life above reproach. I am so blessed to have been given the opportunity to sit at your feet and glean golden nuggets from you both. I know my position in Christ because of you. You talked the talk, but more importantly…you walked it out before us.

- Minister Artra "Mimi" Miller…my friend and covenant sister. Over the years we have walked together through life's dramas and melodramas and have triumphed! You were first to read the pages at the start of this journey. Thank you for being my first critic. I love an appreciate you.

- Michelle Sperber, my "Mishi", prayer warrior and partner…my Jewish sister. Our kindred spirits embraced and rejoiced from the very start. Thank you for sowing into my life, and into my work and for simply having faith in me. The nuggets that you shared were priceless.

- Minister Annette Stewart, my Sistah Soljah. Though three thousand miles away, you encouraged me all the way through my first teaching assignment. I still have the emails that you sent commenting on each lesson and being such a cheer leader. Always giving. I love you

- Pastor Robert L. Cummings, Sr… my "Brudder". You are an earthly example of agape love. Many can testify along with me that your love walk has always been evident and steadfast. You prayed me through and encouraged me through one of the most difficult times in my life. Though thousands of miles were between us, I never felt a gap in your genuine love. You are "one in a kazillion", and I thank God for your presence in my life.

Contents

1. Opportunity Knocks 11
2. The Big Move 14
3. Destiny Delayed 17
4. Fighting A Losing Battle 21
5. Alone and Ashamed 25
6. Showers of Favor 29
7. Out to Save the World 35
8. Satan Sets It Up 45
9. Reeled In 50
10. Cast of Many Faces 56
11. Mega Drama 65
12. Suckered 71
13. Precisioned Deception 80
14. Maximized Mockery 104
15. Major Turn of Events 125
16. Unforgiveness; The Bad Seed 144
17. Doing Church Just Because 151
18. SEE-ming Appealing Can Be De-SEE-ving 177

Foreword

Can the Elect be Deceived?

Can the Elect Be Deceived is a very enlightening and informative book sharing just how the elect can be deceived. Satan has a deceiver in every field and area of life to deceive people. If you are a Christian, he certainly has deceptors stationed around you. That is why we need to continually heed to God's Word, as He says in 1Timothy 4:1-2 "Now the Spirit expressly says that in latter times some will depart from the faith, giving heed to deceiving spirits and doctrines of demons, speaking lies in hypocrisy, having their own conscience seared with a hot iron…"

Nanci C. Nixon has certainly experienced this in her life with several supposed Christians. Firstly, a husband who appeared as a sincere Christian, did everything right for a while, but then the deception manifested when she found out that he was a closet drug addict. Secondly, deception arose in her life after she came across a woman with a small child, who appeared to need help and claimed that her mother as well as others mistreated her. Nanci, being the sincere Christian that she is, basically took care of the woman until deception was clearly seen. She found out that the woman was using her and telling others that she was mistreating her in order to continue to deceive. Thirdly, some ministers, as well as men who deceive their wives are on the "down low." She shares these stories because she experienced most of them and some of the events were shared by others.

I experienced deceivers when it comes to helping and giving to others; sometimes I have given when I should not have. I have also trusted people in my life who were around me just because of whom they thought I was. So when you are a lover of God and people, you need discernment to know why people want to be around you.

This book will help you to observe and know who the deceivers are. It is an easy, nonstop, very interesting and helpful read. Remember – Matthew 24:24 says "For false christs and false prophets will rise and show great signs and wonders to deceive, if possible, even the elect."

My prayer for you is that you will not be deceived.

Dr. Betty R. Price
Crenshaw Christian Center

Introduction

After one of the most devastating experiences in my life, I finally sat down to begin writing the chain of events that left me shaking my head and truly wondering, was it really me that this was happening to? I could be so ashamed to admit my naiveté that I would let this go untold, but it has been stirring in my spirit long enough. In fact, even before I found myself the victim in all of this, I told the perpetrator that this story needed to be told one day, because it was too much like a "LIFETIME" drama in which she appeared to be the victim. Little did I know that I was speaking prophetically.

I began writing what I thought would be the only story of deception in my life. Then God gave me a ministry teaching assignment, which lasted a year and a half. I focused fully on that teaching, and I did not work on this book during that time at all. When I resumed writing the events that occurred years ago, I found myself depending more on Holy Spirit to help me in every aspect. I did not want this to be about me. My desire is for this to be total ministry to others.

As I sat down to write, Abba brought to my remembrance the very first time that I had been deceived after becoming a Christian. He told me to incorporate that experience into this book. I argued with the Lord about this, reminding Him that it had been over twenty years. I asked Him how was I supposed to accurately remember all of the details? At least I had my journals to help tell the current story. He so graciously interrupted my whining fit and repeated what I was to do. Every fiber of my being resisted going back there. I don't know why I thought God would change His mind. Well….He didn't, and as I obeyed Him and began to write the story of twenty years before, every single detail poured out of me like a flood. I had supernatural recall of every thing surrounding that first experience. More than half way through telling that story, He again prompted me, and said that I was to also write about the last experience that I had, which occurred in conjunction with the teaching assignment. All are examples of different kinds of deception that we can innocently and easily fall prey to. I am sure that a great deal of my reading audience can relate, and I imagine that you might even have a few personal stories of your own.

The deceptive influence of the enemy is world wide, and as believers we are not exempt...(Rev. 12:9). In order for prophecy to be fulfilled there will be deception, regardless to whether or not we believe it or accept it. That is the word of God. We are the sanctified; the set apart for God's holy service. We are the elect. The Greek word is elektos; those who have received the gift of God, and have obtained salvation through our Lord, Jesus Christ, and through repentance, have given up the life of sin and turned to Him. Why wouldn't we be the enemy's prime target? He doesn't need to go after the world, he already has them. Satan's last days agenda is to deceive the Body of Christ by any means. Lying signs and wonders will be one of his greatest strategies. These lying signs and wonders cannot be effective unless they sharply resemble the authentic.

Deception doesn't look like itself, much like Satan doesn't look like himself. Scripture says that Satan transforms himself into an angel of light... **2 Corinthians 11:13-14**. That's a lying wonder in itself. An angel of light is quite appealing, so the impostor has to make it look, sound, and feel so authentic that we take the bait.

1.
Opportunity Knocks

My genesis; The City of Brotherly Love shaped the first 37 years of my life. The humid summers I could tolerate, but I always hated the cold and snow. I vowed that I would one day move to a milder climate. Maybe I would end up in the Bahamas, a place where I grew fond of just listening to my mother describe the weather, the beaches and the aquamarine water. Not to mention gazing through the many photos that she took of her annual trip. Mom and her friends vacationed there every year. She always tried to get dad to go, but she couldn't get him to fly at the time. She was adamant about spending her vacation time as far away from home as possible. I liked mom's thinking, that working hard all year deserved more than some R & R in her back yard.

Opportunity knocked after my daughter, Deirdre and my son Derek were both away at college. I was working in North Philly at Freedom Theatre, which was the oldest Black Theatre in town, as Annual Fund Coordinator. That was a real stretch for me. Raising money was not my forte. In addition I was resident actress. Many times I would switch hats in mid-stream, walking out of my office, into the dressing room to prep, then onto the stage. A new season was upon us and guest director, the late Israel Hicks, a professor in the Theatre department at Temple U (my Alma mater), was holding auditions. Our season would open with playwright Charles Fuller's Obie award winning play, "Zooman & the Sign.". My plate was full with planning events for the year, and I really had no interest in auditioning, but the late John Allen, founder and Artistic Director of the Theatre, who was also my first drama instructor, mentor and friend, would came into my office several times during the last few nights of auditions and asked me to think about it. I said, "No" each time, but John had a way of making you feel like you would really miss out. I finally auditioned and ended up with the lead role. When I think back to February 1982, I guess I would have missed out, because what followed would not have happened if I continued to say, "No."

The timing was impeccable. We had just opened with the Obie award winning "Zooman" , and unbeknownst to us Mr. Fuller was about to win the Pulitzer Prize for his latest work. "A Soldier's Story." At Mr. Fuller's request the press conference announcing his latest success would be held at Freedom Theatre. Every newspaper, television and radio station in town showed up. We were definitely in the spotlight right along with the Playwright. From then on we could not accommodate the audiences that crowded into our 120-seat theatre. We started out playing Thursday through Sunday, and ended up with shows seven days a week....even on Monday's when theatres are traditionally dark. Bob Leslie, our General Manager, along with John Allen and our Board of Directors made the decision to step out and move the production to the historical 1100-seat Walnut Street Theatre in downtown Philly. There we could more than accommodate our supporters. Now, in order to attract the numbers that would make this a success, we would need a "name draw." That name would be the late Tony award-winning actress and singer, Ms. Virginia Capers, well celebrated for her talent and charisma., and mostly remembered for her role as "Mama" in the stage production of Lorraine Hansbury's, "A Raisin In the Sun." Ms, Capers flew in from Los Angeles to join the cast of "Zooman", and we had a successful one-month run. As we exchanged good-byes and well wishes with Ms. Capers, she and I also exchanged numbers, but I never expected what would happen next. She was so impressed with our cast and the script that she decided to produce the show in Los Angeles. One day as I was in my office wading through paperwork, I received a call from her offering me an airline ticket to come and play the character of my original role for her. The actress that she had cast was not working out. My buddy, Johnnie Hobbs, Jr., who played the role of my husband was offered the same opportunity, but because he was married it took him a few extra days to get clearance. I jumped at the chance. I put things in order and announced the news to my boss who sent me off with his blessings.

The flight was less than five hours, and I arrived in Los Angeles reeling with excitement. The airport was huge in comparison to Philadelphia International. I followed the signs that would lead me to baggage claim, and as I started down the escalator I focused on the great wall in front of me that sported a life sized colored photo of then Mayor Tom Bradley. That was pretty impressive. Virginia met me at baggage claim with that winning smile of hers. The drive from the airport was a sight to behold. I thought, "What a beautiful city." The palm trees lined every street, the sun was beaming, the street names were intriguing, and everything looked prosperous and promising. Even the so-called ghetto looked plush and green. Of course, that's a "first impression", but nevertheless, for me it too was an impressive sight.

Virginia drove straight to the Gene Dynarski Theatre in Hollywood where the show would open in two weeks. I sat and watched the rehearsal which was already in progress. After rehearsal I was introduced to the cast. I blended right in and we all had a great working relationship. I learned that theatre had not yet caught on in LA., which is of course, primarily a film and TV town.

After being in Los Angeles for one month, I was not ready to return home. Virginia introduced us to the cream of the crop in the industry, and spoiled us with lavish outings, meals, recreation and gifts. When her schedule was full there was always someone willing to fill in. I knew without a doubt that I would come back here to live. Not for this awesome experience alone, but because it was what I had dreamed of above all. Someplace where there was no cold, and no snow! Hallelujah! I didn't have to leave the country and move to the Bahamas after all.

2.
The Big Move

In April of 1984 I sold, stored and packed my belongings and drove my two-toned blue 1977 Ford Maverick cross-country to Los Angeles, California. My friend, Tom who had lived in LA for years, drove with me. My dad wasn't very vocal, but my mom thought I had lost my mind. Our family was close. I was very close to my mom, so it didn't seem natural to her that I would be serious about moving all the way across the country. My friend, Jan who lived in the San Fernando Valley, had asked me for years to come to Los Angeles, so this was my ticket. We took the northern route through the Rocky Mountains, and the scenery was awesome! Natural architecture sculpted the mountains into statues and forms unlike anything I had ever seen. Tom had a friend who was a disc jockey in Denver, Colorado, so when we got there we were invited to spend the night. His friend gave us our first introduction to the compact disc. He told us that the CD would be replacing audiotapes. Looking at that flat, round silver disc I found that hard to believe back then, but.... oh, well. Over thirty years later and the disc is still here.

After leaving Denver, we finally got to Nevada and spent a night in the desert sleeping in the car under stars that looked like thousands of diamonds against a coal black sky. The stars seemed so close...like you could reach up and gather them in baskets. We had a great trip and finally arrived in California on May 5th...my first introduction to Cinco de Mayo. Tom dropped me off at Jan's in the Valley and drove to Hollywood where he would be staying with some old friends. It was Friday evening a little before 6:00 p.m. when I arrived. Jan was cooking dinner and waiting for her favorite pastor (whom she wanted me to watch) to come on TV. I didn't know that I was about to meet my future pastor via television. I didn't know that my life was about to be changed forever. I wasn't saved yet, so watching him was something that I did mostly to appease her. After all, I had just arrived in sunny California. I had places to go, people to meet and a career to launch.

One day before Tom left to go back to Philly, he introduced me to his friends, Keith and Gilda Leos, a young couple who lived in Hollywood and whose pastor just happened to be…guess who? You got it! He was the same man that I was watching on TV at Jan's house. Talk about Divine destiny! They were members of his church, and immediately invited me to attend a service with them sometime. I said that I would but did not make any promises as to when. We exchanged numbers and kept in touch. In fact, I moved within two months and got an apartment about ten blocks from them. We became good friends.They never badgered me about going to church, but they reminded me from time to time that they would be happy to pick me up and take me when I was ready. It took me six months to get ready, but one Saturday night I called, and Gilda answered the phone. I asked her if they would pick me up for church in the morning. She was ecstatic and for some reason I was a bit excited too. I certainly had no idea what to expect. I just knew that I was ready to go. Bright and early the next morning my new found friends picked me up. We chatted all the way, and when we arrived there was a long line of people midway down the block waiting to get in. In order to accommodate the people, the pastor did three services each Sunday. We were attending the second service. This was new and strange, but I didn't mind. I remember thinking," There must be something good about all of this." I had never in my life neither seen nor heard of people standing in line to get into a church.

I later found out that the auditorium where service was held seated about 1,000 people. Yet, when the pastor began teaching I felt like I was inside of a box and there was no one in that box except God, that pastor and me. All of those people didn't matter. This wasn't church as usual. He walked around teaching from the bible which he held in his hand, and he had everyone following along. I didn't know what that "swishing" sound was, but I found out later that it was all of those bible pages turning in unison. Generally I would have been petrified to stand up before a crowd, but when the sermon was over the pastor gave four invitations; to receive Jesus as Savior and Lord, to receive the gift of the Holy Spirit with the evidence of speaking in other tongues, assurance of salvation, and church membership. I was on my feet in a flash! I didn't think twice. I knew without a doubt that I needed one of those things, if not all of them. When he told us to move to the nearest aisle and follow the instructions of the ushers, I did not hesitate. I remember him praying, and then shaking each of our hands. The next thing I knew, I was in the prayer room being ministered to by a counselor who asked if I knew which invitation I responded to. She laughed when I shrugged my shoulders and told her, "Probably all of them." After ascertaining my spiritual condition, she took me through several scriptures. I followed along as she read and explained what the scriptures meant, but Romans 10:9-10 stood out most to me. Afterwards, she had me repeat what is known as "the sinner's prayer" after her. She then introduced me to the Holy Spirit and asked if I wanted to receive the gift with the evidence of speaking in my heavenly language. I said, "Yes" without hesitating. I wanted everything that God had for me and I didn't want to put anything off for later. After being filled with the Holy Spirit and speaking in other tongues, I was encouraged to pray in my heavenly language every day for at least ten minutes and that after I felt comfortable I should increase it. I was so impressed with how this lady ministered to me that I knew I would someday do the same. I could not wait until my one-year membership had come to pass. Then I could work in the Helps Ministry. The seed was planted that day. I wanted to lead people to the Lord.

3.
Destiny Delayed

My desire to be a part of Helps Ministry as a counselor was delayed by years because of my first encounter with deception. Just before I reached my one-year mark I met the man who would be my husband. I was eleven months old in the Lord and Juan was eleven years old in the Lord. We met while I was taking my daily walk and he was riding his bike on one of my favorite trails in the Echo Mountains of Altadena. He was a handsome man, quite distinguished and friendly, not to mention easy to talk to. After establishing that we were both Christians, we had even more to talk about. That first day after finishing our exercise, we sat on a wall at the entrance of the forest and talked for over an hour about nothing but the things of God. When he found out what church I went to, he said that he always wanted to visit. I immediately invited him to come along sometimes. He shared about the things that he had acquired over the years, but how as a result of backsliding, Satan had ripped him off. He said he lost everything and was starting all over. He was a collector of '55 Chevys and had a '55 Chevy car and truck. He had a good job as a builder and contractor. We exchanged numbers and that's how it all began. I had already begun making plans to go home for the holidays. I always got my airline ticket early at a great price. I was also about to mark my one-year anniversary as a member of the church. Now I could apply for the Helps Ministry! One day as we were talking on the phone about the things of God Juan let me know that he always wanted to get married. I didn't know it, but Satan was setting me up. Once he found out that I had gotten my ticket to go home, the pressure was on and, "Let's get married" was his daily song. He wanted to go with me, but he knew that it couldn't happen otherwise. I wanted to be married too, but I also wanted this to be right. Even as a young Christian I knew that it was too soon. I held my ground for two months, but finally I folded under the pressure. And if the truth be told, it was flattering to have this man constantly asking me to marry him and telling me all of the reasons why we should and that we both "Know it's of God." I realized later.....much later that I was infatuated, not in love. I was impressed by a man whom I thought loved God, knew His Word, and was now re-committed to doing that Word. I was going to marry a spiritual giant! There was so much pressure from him to hurry and marry that I didn't even go to my pastor or any of the pastoral staff for counseling. What did I know? A pre-marital counseling session never crossed my mind, so consequently I yielded to the spirit of deception.

We went to a chapel in Las Vegas to get married. I didn't even buy a new dress. I chose a pink silk dress that I had only worn once, styled my hair in an up-sweep and put a cluster of baby's breath in it. I was not feeling good about this and I didn't have the guts to call it off. Holy Spirit was trying to save me from making a drastic mistake, but I was not spiritually mature enough to discern that. I called my mom and told her that we were on the way to Vegas. I didn't tell her how nervous and pressured I felt. I had told her all about Juan and she was excited about the proposal. Mom and I talked about us marrying so soon but justified it by remembering other marriages that had worked out just fine with short courtships.

Juan and I had a big argument on the way to Las Vegas. This would be my final warning by Holy Spirit. Yes, that's right. Final warning! You see there had been quite a few previous warnings. Our Father always alerts His children. We don't always obey, but Abba never leaves His children wandering. Discernment is always available to us. I did not yield to the warnings of Holy Spirit but, oh how I wished I had.

The irony of it all was that my pastor had just begun teaching a series on the Christian Family. Beginning with marriage and divorce, pastor followed by teaching on the duties of the husband, duties of the wife, the children, and the parents. He told us that if we could hang in there for nine or ten weeks while he taught the series, it would serve as one big counseling session for everyone. At the beginning of each subject pastor encouraged our participation by asking us to write down our individual questions or situations. He would then address them in the service, and as a congregation we could receive ministry and counseling all at once. This unique method took about 40 weeks, and it was awesome! But by the time he got to "the duties of the husband" and "the duties of the wife", my marriage was on the rocks. Before we were married, my husband was in church with me every Sunday. Sound familiar? To my dismay I found that I had married a closet drug abuser. He had actually been delivered from heroine years before and showed me the nearly invisible track marks on his arms. What I didn't know was that he was daily using crack cocaine. I wasn't wise to the habits of a drug user, although I had been exposed to their reputation as liars, manipulators, and thieves. Every family has been exposed in some way to the behaviors and tactics of a loved one, a friend, or a neighbor on drugs. Mine was no exception. However, with my husband, I never saw strange behavior or any paraphernalia that would give me the slightest hint that he was doing drugs. Then I remembered the time that we were about to leave for Philly. He gave me money to pick out a couple of outfits and a winter coat for him to take. In the meantime, he would get paid that evening and he told me that he would pay a few bills and get some shoes. When he finally got home, he was excited about his purchases and took them out to show me. He had good taste. The sweaters were a little on the pricey side, but they were nice, so I didn't quip. Then he gave me $600.00 and told me to hold on to it. I knew there should be much more and when I asked him about it he attempted to account for the missing pieces of the puzzle. He went over and over what he had spent, reaching into his pockets and turning them inside out several times as if he expected the missing cash to appear. He looked puzzled as he tried hard to come up with what could have happened to the missing cash. I remember getting a check in my spirit, but with all of the excitement, I finally dismissed it, just as I did the other times that Holy Spirit warned me. Of course, I can say this now, but I truly did not know until it was all over that it was Holy Spirit trying to save me from this grief.

We stayed in my home town for three weeks. Juan said and did all the right things. He bought gifts, took my family out to the finest restaurants, and the favorite thing to do was horseback riding. He made a winning impression on my family and on me. He loved to street witness and was bold in doing so. He even gave me money to buy blankets and coats for the homeless for Christmas. We went out on the streets and I mostly watched as he boldly ministered Jesus to every potential candidate. There were times when I was tired and he would go out by himself. Our cash was getting thin, but of course I believed that he was feeding someone in the streets. After we ran out of cash I got advances on my credit card, confident that it would be okay. After all, money was no option. He would pay the credit card off as soon as we got back home.

4.
Fighting A Losing Battle

We had just returned home when I met my sister in-law, Dinah for the first time. We liked each other right away. She was a comical lady with a big mouth and no inhibitions. She and her husband had three daughters and I soon began to see the kind of family that I had married into. My husband had shared that he was from a large family (17 siblings). His mother was married now to her fourth husband and had not been married to Juan's father. I learned from him that most of his siblings were not upright people. In fact, there was only one brother that I met who was fondly spoken of. He made himself scarce and seemed to be set apart from the rest. Two other brothers and their wives were into car insurance scams. They looked for people driving expensive cars and would cut them off and stop suddenly which would cause a rear end collision. Of course, they would cry injury so they could collect on the person's insurance. Juan told me of the brutal murder of his older sister by her husband. The two younger sisters were both on drugs and one was involved in a homosexual relationship. Another sister would scam apartment owners and move every four to six months to keep from paying rent. I found out that his mother held the purse that made change for the drug dealers. I saw this with my own eyes when I had gone to meet Juan at his mother's one evening. The living room was full of people that I did not know. He ushered me into his mother's bedroom where she and her husband sat propped on their pillows in bed watching TV. The room was very spacious, and they invited me to have a seat in a fancy chair while I waited for Juan. What I witnessed next both sickened and infuriated me. The bathroom was attached to their bedroom and after I was there about ten minutes, Juan's baby sister came through to the bathroom followed by a guy. They both went in and in a matter of minutes they came out. The sister handed mother a bill and she reached under her pillow, took out what looked like a drawstring purse and made change. I saw this three times within thirty minutes. I knew that Juan and I were going to have words because he had put me in a situation that was uncomfortable, unsafe and unethical. I was beside myself. This is proof that is so important to know the character of the person and of the family that you are marrying into, especially if you plan to have children. Thank God that was not in my plan. What a shattering thought that I might have brought a child into such dysfunction because I didn't take the time to know for myself what kind of man and family I was about to link up with. Children are innocent, but all too often they end up being the victims and paying for our selfish desires and thoughtless mistakes.

Juan was a high-functioning addict. He got up every morning and went to work without a problem. He was always on time and never missed a day. He encouraged me to pursue my acting career if that's what I wanted. He even offered to pay my dues to join the actors union. At that time, it was only $800.00 to join. I foolishly did not take advantage of it then, because I thought I could take my time; I had nothing to be concerned about.

Sunday after Sunday I went to church alone. I was so torn up inside. Though I was seeing what a grave mistake I had made, I was determined to make my marriage work. I did not want to fail, but things only got worse. Suddenly Juan didn't want to the pay bills and began staying away from home on his payday. I took me a minute to realize this, but it dawned on me that he would pick a fight every Wednesday night so that when he got paid on Thursday, he would feel justified in not coming home. When I saw what he was doing I refused to engage him, which only made matters worse. He would find something wrong and go off on a lone tangent. I knew then that I was fighting a losing battle, because he was not willing to take responsibility for his actions. He would pollute his body with drugs, but only wanted me to buy the healthiest food products. When I bought everything on the list, but had spent over what he thought I should, there was another argument. Well, eating healthy cost a bit more, but he could not hear that.

One day my sister in-law called and jokingly asked if Juan was treating me right.

My silence confirmed her suspicion. She told me that she knew her brother and knew what he was doing. Then she spat it out, "He's doing those drugs and that is why he wouldn't introduce us before you got married." She said, "I did not want to see a woman's life ruined, because I'm a woman too." She was angry and went on to say... 'You might have hated me for telling you the truth, but if we had met beforehand, I would have warned you, and the rest would be your decision." Dinah told me how her brother used to rent a back house at the property that she and her husband once had. She said that they could hear him starting his car every few hours throughout the night, going back and forth to get drugs; yet he always went to work and always paid on time. They knew what he was doing, but never confronted him.

Things didn't get any better. I confronted him about the drugs, but he only said and did what drug users say and do. It's always manipulative and always what they think you want to hear. He continued to stay away from home on pay day, but would call home like clock work on Sunday night, remorseful and apologetic, "forgive me, I love you, I'm so sorry.", and constantly giving some conjured up excuse for his behavior. I did not know which path to take. I prayed the best I knew how and hoped for a change. Finally, I knew that I had to make the change. Four months into my marriage I made up my mind that I was not going to continue along this path. I was not a doormat and no matter how much I wanted this marriage to work, I had to love myself more than I loved what I was holding on to. I had had enough! I decided that he had picked his last fight with me.

His truck was smoking terribly and had stopped running. I took him to work that morning knowing that he would not be back that night because it was payday. I knew it would be at least three days before I would hear from him. I returned home and began packing his belongings. I called his sister, Dinah because his '55 Chevy car was sitting in her yard. It wasn't running either, but those cars are huge inside and I knew that it would hold everything that he owned. I told her what I was doing and asked if the car was locked. She said, "yes", but the key was accessible. I was on my way. I loaded my Maverick to the brim and somehow, I even got his bike on top of my car so that I could make one trip. I did not want to leave anything behind that would give him a reason to come back to the apartment. Dinah lived in Highland Heights and we lived in the Silver Lake area of LA, so the trip wasn't too long. Dinah was very supportive and in total agreement with my decision. When I pulled up in her yard she met me with the key, and without guilt or remorse I got busy loading the car with his belongings.

I knew that he would get the news within a day or so, because he still hung out in that area. I knew that Dinah would get the word to him in plenty of time.

I finished the task at hand and hurried home to have the locks changed on the doors. I had peace at last, and I slept like a baby that night for the first time in months.

5.
Alone and Ashamed

I spent the next few days praying and watching Christian television. I had a chance to reflect. I began remembering all of the times that Holy Spirit had warned me and I felt compelled to write each one down. There were eleven times altogether. I remember thinking…" What an odd number." I tried to think of at least twelve times, but to this day I have never been able to come up with a different number. I thought it was so strange. That number "11" showed up again and again. I tried to make sense of it; eleven warnings, eleven years, (Juan had been saved)…eleven months, (I had been saved). Curiosity caused me to look at biblical mathematics and I discovered that eleven is the number of judgment, and judgment comes after many warnings. I was so despondent because of the way things had turned out. I felt like a loser, even though I finally had peace.

During that time, I learned a lot about people who are challenged with drug abuse. Within the next few weeks two young men who were celebrities died of drug related incidents. I had not understood my husband's thinking and I needed answers. I believe God answered my prayer and directed me to watch a documentary one night that answered so many of my questions. The young man who was telling his story about severe drug dependency helped me to understand the dynamics that are involved and that are such a stronghold. He said, "The temporary euphoria keeps one believing that the intensity and the feeling of the high they are experiencing will continue and be even greater each time. {Deception} It never delivers, and consequently the ongoing struggle to remain enraptured causes impaired judgment, which can only lead to destruction." The young man expressed his inability to stop the downward spiral as he lost his job, then his home, his wife and children, relationships with his his family members and friends, and ultimately his own self. He said, "You become that drug, and you are no longer your own." I could identify with that because I watched that drug become wife to my husband. He was truly "romancing the stone." I felt like the "other woman." I came to realize that I could not and would not compete. After watching the documentary, I suddenly acquired some insight. I began to understand why my husband could not control his behavior. The crack was in control and he was not his own.

Now I needed to talk to someone about my decision. I called my church and got an appointment with my pastor's wife and I told her everything. In her most gracious and assuring way, she first gave me the Word of God in Mat. 19:6, which says: "What God has joined together, let no man separate." Then she broke it down to help me understand that while marriage is God's institution and is ordained of God, sometimes He has never been sought and therefore is nowhere around when we make some of the decisions that get us into trouble. When it was all said and done, I understood completely that God had not joined Juan and me together. In fact, God, by His Spirit tried everything to keep me from being joined together with a man who would deceive me.

I desperately needed a job. I had already gotten advances on my credit card and now I needed to get another advance to keep roof overhead. Both of my kids were in college, so I was paying rent times three; their dorm fees plus my rent. In desperation I began looking at positions as a resident manager. I knew that I could possibly work outside, manage a building and have my rent free, or at the very least at a discount. After researching my options, I chose to go with a management company that upon completing their classes offered placement at one of their many buildings. In the interim I had to do the thing that I dreaded most, and that was to call my parents and borrow part of the next month's rent. Another good friend sent me one hundred dollars and together with the final cash advance, my rent was paid.

One evening as I was driving to my residential management class I got a second witness that helped me to know that moving on was the best decision that I could make. I was listening to Christian radio and a well-known pastor was giving advice to married couples. He turned his attention to women who were suffering different kinds of abuse, and said that he was not advocating divorce, but sometimes you need to adhere to Prov.14:7 which says: "Separate yourself from the foolish man," This was my confirmation and from that day on I had total peace about my decision and the direction that I would need to take.

I wanted desperately to be involved in the Ministry of Helps at my church but found that my marital status presented a challenge. In order to work in the Ministry of Helps at that time, you had to either be reconciled, reconciling with your spouse or divorced. I was neither, but I knew what my next step would be. I needed to make a clean break, so I made up my mind to divorce my husband. I figured it would be pretty easy since it was obvious that he did not want to be married. Little did I know that this would take at least three years! Juan was very angry that I had made the move to separate from him, so he decided to make my life as miserable as he possibly could. I knew that I did not have the money to file for a divorce, so I did my research. I found that I could go to the courthouse and pick up the necessary documents to file for marriage dissolution and that is what I did. The next step was to figure out how to properly document all information. I was warned that one misplaced word could cause the paperwork to be rejected and the process to be delayed. I was directed to the law library a few blocks away from the court. There was a manual on "How to do your own dissolution." You were not allowed to take it out of the library, but you could sign it out for two hours at a time. I set up camp at the law library and signed that manual out every two hours for at least six hours a day. I lost track of how many times I traveled down town to the law library, but I did not have a choice. I had difficulty understanding the jargon that was used in some cases and needed to study this thing out so that I could complete every document as accurately as possible. I studied intensely and when I finally got everything completed, it was time to have Juan served with the divorce papers.

Super challenge number two! In Los Angeles at that time, you could get the sheriff's department to serve legal documents free of charge. They would attempt to serve a total of three times, Monday through Friday between the hours of 6:00 a.m. and 1:00 p.m. The odds appeared to be against me. Juan had to be at work by 6:00 a.m. and he was not off until 5:00 p.m. Knowing this, I still allowed them to try and serve him. I didn't have anything to lose. I was hopeful that maybe he would take a day off or go in late. The sheriff's department tried three times, but to no avail. I felt so helpless… literally like a trained yo-yo. I could not believe the position that I found myself in. This man was controlling my life and I could not do a thing about it. I exhausted all options to find someone else who could serve him, since it was against the law to have a family member involved with the serving process. When his sister, Dinah called to say that he had been arrested, I got another glimmer of hope. She gave me all of the information and I immediately mailed the papers. By the time they reached their destination, Juan had posted bail and been released. The papers didn't come back to me until three weeks later. When I received my mail that day and saw the envelope marked, "Undeliverable" I got a hollow, sick feeling in the pit of my stomach. I cried out, "O God…when will this be over?"

6.
Showers of Favor

After completion of my classes with the management company it was not long before I received placement as a residential manager. I inherited a property that had several vacancies to be cleaned. A Christian lady who owned one of the maintenance companies did excellent work, but she was always booked up. I really needed to get the vacancies ready ASAP, but I learned from other managers that some of the other vendors were not as reliable. I decided to chance it and call her number. Bingo! I was told that she could have a crew out to me by early afternoon. She showed up with her crew but stayed in my apartment talking the entire time. Somehow, we got on the subject about marriage and I found myself telling her the whole story of my situation. I know that God sent that angel to me. She was a paralegal by profession and worked for a well-established law firm. I was astounded and ecstatic at the same time when she told me to get his information and that she would serve him for me free of charge and with no strings attached.

By now I found out that Juan had moved, and no one knew where he was. He also knew that I was trying to serve him divorce papers, so he was more evasive than ever. This is unheard of today, but at that time if you were searching for someone, you could go to the DMV with that person's name and social security number, and they would issue a printout with their current address on it. My paralegal angel informed me of this when I told her that I did not have a clue where he was. It was like going on a treasure hunt. I was so excited! This was finally my answer and I knew that this was a God sent opportunity to be free of this bondage.

I was up bright and early the next morning. DMV's in Los Angeles were always crowded, especially in the mornings. My hands were clammy, and my heart was racing as I walked into the DMV and followed the signs directing me to the first line. After about twenty minutes I heard the lady say, "Next in line." My legs couldn't carry me fast enough. I explained what I needed and gave her the necessary information. She ran the information through a couple of times, then looked at me and said, "I can't pick it up here." She turned to a co-worker and conversed with her showing my request. I was directed to another line that was for troubleshooting. She told me that the gentleman there was more likely to help me. My stomach began churning, but I held on to my faith as I prayed softly. I got to the other side where I was fourth in line. Now the drama begins. There was a couple in front of me that was not happy, and they were going at it with the gentleman that I was supposed to see. Back and forth they went, and I could see the clerk getting more agitated. I thought..." Great, by the time I get up there he'll be so ticked off that he won't want to help me." As that issue was being resolved, a lady standing in the line next to mine began having a seizure. I would be lying if I told you that I didn't have the selfish thought, "Why now, Lord? Of course everyone began to gather and stare as she was placed onto the floor assisted by a security officer. By now my heart was palpitating. The lady was frothing at the mouth and shaking uncontrollably as medical attention arrived and security asked everyone to stay back. By now I was next in line, watching my guy adopt a new disposition. In retrospect a scripture comes to mind, "All things work together for good to them that love God, to them who are called according to His purpose." (Rom. 8:28). Sometimes we can't see the good in catastrophe, in upheaval, in interference, or in opposition, and the list goes on. But if we believe God, then we must look for and ultimately see things working for our good, and for His Glory! The trials and tribulations that we face in life are not only for us to mature and be strengthened by. They help and encourage others. To quote my late beloved mentor and friend, Pastor Milt Jackson, "You cannot have a testimony without first having a test." I had to adopt the above scripture as a daily reminder that no matter what was happening; it had to be for my good, and for His glory. Who knows except God the things that were taking place or even prevented by the circumstance of that lady's physical challenge at that specific time? I witnessed the irate couple calm down, and consequently there was a domino effect.

I was called next, and when I gave the clerk my request he was courteous, calm and collected. He turned to his computer and within seconds whipped out the information that I needed. I could hardly contain myself. I couldn't wait to get home and call my paralegal angel with the news. I was so blessed to have this woman in my corner.

It was a long haul and at least five tries before Juan was successfully served. After her third try I felt so bad, but she encouraged me and assured me that we would get it done. I would scrape up what I could and try to pay her, but she would not accept it. Finally I did get her to agree to let me take her to dinner. This woman would drive from her home near the LAX airport to Altadena where Juan now lived. The drive is about forty-five to fifty miles round trip. I recognized the favor of the Lord in operation, because I have experienced His favor so many times over the years. On her fifth attempt to serve Juan, I sat by the phone praying and waiting for the call. The call came at approximately 8:45 p.m. The minute I answered the phone, and before a word was spoken I felt a release like a starburst explode in my spirit. It was done! I was told that Juan responded in disbelief that I had finally located his whereabouts after nearly three years. In the next six months I would be free to go on with my life.

It seemed like forever, but six months was up, and my divorce was final. I was scheduled for my morals interview at church so that I could start working in Helps Ministry. My heart was to minister salvation and Holy Spirit to the people responding to the invitations that our pastor gave at the end of each service. After completing my interview, I began the classes that were offered and completed my training. I became a counselor (personal ministry worker) and I was so excited when I successfully ministered to my first respondent. I did not know that I had a call on my life at the time. I only knew that I had a passion to see people come to the saving knowledge of Jesus Christ and be filled with the power of Holy Spirit with the evidence of speaking with other tongues, which is the real prayer language. I attended bible studies, Women's fellowships, conventions, retreats, and every other function at our church. I could not get enough of the rich wholesome ministry of the Word of God. I gathered all kinds of tapes and books. I was hungry and craved more and more spiritual food.

During my fourth year of counseling in the personal ministries auxiliary, I realized that my appetite for the things of God was increasing even more. I thought about taking some of the spiritual enrichment classes that were offered through the church but decided against it. My reason was that the classes offered tons of information, but there were no books required or exams given, so there was no way for me to measure my advancement. One Saturday I was in my office at our acting studio when my friend Rowena, whom I had not seen in awhile came by. I asked where she had been, and she told me, "In school." When I asked "where", she told me that she had started classes at our Ministry Training Institute the month before. As we began to talk more, she actually ministered to me. She told me that I was a teacher and that she didn't know why I wasn't in school. My daughter who was teaching a class downstairs happened to run into the office to get something from a file and chimed in on the conversation to "ditto" what my friend was saying. Later that night, Rowena called me at home to continue our conversation and convince me that I needed to go on Monday and inquire about the School of Ministry. After going back and forth as to why I shouldn't go right now, I promised her that I would at least check it out, and I did.

I was a bit excited as well as anxious, because I didn't know what to expect.

I walked into the MTI office and words cannot transcend the chain of events that followed. First, all protocol seemed to disappear for a season. I announced that I was there to speak with someone about the School of Ministry. The vague look that I got followed by the information that the school had already been in session for over a month, told me that I should just forget it. Then I heard the words, "Who would you like to speak to?" Even though I knew that one must have an appointment to see any of the pastors, I found myself mouthing Dean Landry's name. The secretary turned to me, hunched her shoulders and said, "Ok". She walked out of the office and returned in a matter of minutes with the dean following her. He had on his blue smock, which meant that it wasn't a ministry day for him, but a different kind of workday. In his most gracious and kind way, he smiled and said, "How may I help you?" I repeated my reason for being there and he proceeded to fill me in on the details. He told me how much I had already missed and what I needed to catch up on, including passed due response papers and reading assignments, book reports; also several quizzes were coming up in certain classes and mid-terms were close. In the first trimester there were six classes and of course each instructor expected all assignments to be completed on time. Major points were lost if assignments were late. While he was talking to me, my friend, Rowena who was also employed at the church in children's ministry, came to the office and as she opened the door and saw me, we both became emotional. When we had collected ourselves and asked his pardon, Dean Landry ushered me into his office where he began to minister to me concerning my decision. I remember thinking…"This is totally against protocol." I didn't even have an appointment. I'll never forget his words as he offered me a seat. He said, "Young lady, when I am dressed like this (referring to the smock) I am up to my elbows with work, not ministry. I started not to see you today, but the Lord impressed upon my heart that I was supposed to." After a lengthy interview, Dean Landry presented the options of attending day or evening classes. I decided that day classes would be the best fit for me. After giving me more insight about the school, he asked if I was ready to sit in on the classes in session for that day. I was ready. From his bookshelves he handed me the text for each of the classes and one of his many bibles, then walked with me to the first class. He introduced me to the instructor and left, instructing me to leave everything with his secretary if he was not in when I was done.

I wasn't allowed to be a spectator. I ended up participating in the classes, but at the end, I was undecided if I should do this now, or wait and start afresh the next year. I would be nearly six weeks behind in every class. I was concerned about catching up, and I did not want to do less than my best. I also knew that the longer I put it off, the more reasons that I would find to further put it off. Immediately I thought of the tuition, the books, and the tapes from each class. I would need these immediately to catch up. There were mid-terms coming up and I knew that I needed to hear, process, and decipher the information from each of these six classes. I became overwhelmed just thinking about it. I decided to write Dean Landry a note letting him know that I needed to think about it.

I didn't have to think about it too long. The favor of God began to fall all around me. Once at home I called my friend Royce Wallace, a veteran actress and told her that I was thinking about going to ministry school. She got so excited. After telling me how wonderful she thought it was, she asked how much it was going to cost. When I gave her the amount of the first installment, she asked, "When are you coming to pick it up?" Wow!

That was the beginning of the many blessings that began to flow. Audiotapes and notes for the classes were loaned to me, books were bought for me, and tuition was paid for me. I was able to catch up on the five papers that were due from each class, take and pass a mid-term being given on my first day in one of the classes, complete five out of six reading assignments, and maintain an A/B average for all mid-terms and final exams. And yes, I am bragging on my Father! He showed Himself mightily!! I was voted class representative and at graduation two years later I received the Faculty Award for Excellence in Leadership. None of it came without some challenges. It was not easy, but it was all quite rewarding.

7.
Out to Save the World

Fresh out of ministry school, I was out to save the world. I believe a lot of us ministers make the grave mistake of thinking that we are supposed to rescue every damsel and gent in distress. We find out the hard way that our well of supply is not sufficient to meet the needs of the people. Only God's well of plenty runs deep enough, wide enough, and is a continuous flow of more than enough.

I remember doing my first sermon in ministry school and right in the middle of my presentation, the Holy Spirit spoke to me and said, "Ask them if the elect can be deceived?" I paused almost in disbelief, but went on to be obedient and did as the Spirit of God had said. In unison everyone answered, "Yes." Then Holy Spirit said to ask: "Are we the elect?" I asked, and like a chorus once again, everyone answered, "Yes." As He gave me the words, I said: "Then we can be deceived." When the following fiasco was all over and I had time to reflect, those very words and the day that I spoke them out of my mouth to my fellow classmates, came back to haunt me. "**Can the elect be deceived? Are we the elect? Then we can be deceived.**" It is my desire that some will be ministered to, some will become free, some because of reading this will be saved just in the nick of time from making the same mistakes, but all will see and perhaps experience God's keeping power.

When I met Vivien Alston we were both relief counselors at a residential treatment program for the adult mentally challenged. There were two facilities about a mile apart. I had been there five years and worked between both places, as I was needed. For about two months I noticed her name on the register of new hires at the smaller location. I finally met her when the person I usually worked with had an emergency and Vivien was asked to fill in. When she arrived we introduced ourselves and she told me that she heard a lot of good things about me. It was October and as we engaged in small talk, a common bond was immediately discovered in our dislike for the extravagant Halloween decorations of skulls, bones, goblins, spider webs, and the likes. After all, we were both Christians and the celebration of death just wasn't a welcome sight. I found out that she worked full-time at a small private school as a third grade teacher, and that her daughter attended the school where she was employed.

Our shift ended at midnight and as we walked to our cars together we wished each other a good night and a safe trip home. A week later I was scheduled for the smaller facility and when I arrived everything was chaotic. They needed a full audience at one of the big movie studios in Hollywood for one of the new shows, and our program director had volunteered the residents of both facilities to fill those seats. Viv (as she liked to be called) and I would be working together again. We were instructed to go to the main facility, pick up the residents and drop them off at the movie studio where other staff would be waiting to receive them. We were further instructed to go to the smaller facility and pick up all residents there. Just as this was done and we were back at the facility preparing meds and charting, we received a call to go back to the movie studios and pick up all residents and take them back to their respective housing. The audience had been overbooked and there were no seats for our residents. Well, that gave us plenty to talk about as we got acquainted. The director was not very popular among staff to begin with, and now sending us on a wild goose chase in an attempt to obtain peanut revenue did not help her popularity.

The following week Viv and I worked together again. This time she wasn't feeling well when she came in and complained of a headache. I took the shift alone and told her to sit in the back office and put her head down on the desk until time to dispense the meds. Before our shift ended she seemed to feel better and came out into the main office to chat. She asked where I attended church, and seemed excited when I told her. She said that she had come to my church once, but that her mom wasn't fond of large churches, so she never returned. She spoke highly of my Pastor saying, "We need more teachers like him in the Body of Christ." After the residents settled down for the night, we spent the final hour of our shift talking mainly about the things of God. She asked a lot of questions about things that she didn't understand. That was right up my alley. I enjoyed sharing and she seemed quite interested. As the conversation shifted she mentioned that she wanted an extra curricular activity for her five year old daughter. At that time my daughter, Deirdre and I had an acting studio. We trained youth in the performing arts and showcased their talents every twelve weeks. We were always looking to bless a child with a scholarship, either because their parents couldn't afford the fees or because they had worked hard and deserved it. I told her all about our school and invited her to come down and bring her daughter the following weekend to the orientation for new students. She promised that she would.

We were scheduled to work together the following Friday, but Viv didn't come in. I realized that I was going to be doing the shift alone and one of the residents informed me that Viv was sick and in the hospital. I was concerned and I remembered that she wasn't feeling well the last time that we worked together. I didn't have a phone number for her, so it was another week before I found her number in the employees contact file and called her during my shift. She couldn't believe that I had taken the time to call her. She began to cry on the phone and told me that she was so touched that anyone would think enough of her to call and check on her. She told me that she was a diabetic and that she had been in the hospital because her sugar had been so high that she went into a diabetic comma. She told me that she and her daughter would have to miss the orientation scheduled for the next day. I assured her that it was okay and that we would reschedule for another time.

It was coming up on the holiday season and the next couple of months were a busy time for Deirdre and me. Between the planning of our annual fall production, getting our massive mailing off for the upcoming winter session, and planning our holiday trip to Philly to see our family for Christmas, I saw very little of Viv. She often seemed depressed and it appeared to be a hardship for her to get her child to the studio for an interview, which was necessary to begin classes. One of the reasons that she gave was that her mother was strict and did not agree with Viv's choice of any activity for her child that was not church related. From the things that she shared I came to the conclusion that they were constantly at odds.

One Saturday afternoon before I left to go home for the holidays I invited Viv over and asked her to bring her daughter so that I could meet her. Viv and Babbi came to visit. She was a pretty little girl, though a bit over dressed for a Saturday afternoon, and quite inquisitive. A short time into our visit I could tell that she needed the discipline that we taught our students at the studio. We had a nice visit and decided that it would be best for Babbi to start classes when we returned after the New Year.

Upon my return Viv and I didn't work together too much at the beginning of the New Year. It was 1999, and we had a new program manager who cut hours, showed favoritism, and sided with manipulative residents. This would be my final year working in the mental health field.

When Viv and I weren't working together she would either come by the facility where I was or often times I would get a call at home asking if she could come by. If she was working, she would drop the residents off for their AA or CA meetings that were usually around 90 minutes, and then she would head to my place. She seemed so interested in knowing more about the things of God. She constantly told me that she wished she were a part of a teaching ministry, because she didn't feel as though she was being fed the Word of God. She asked lots of biblical questions and was especially interested in learning of Holy Spirit. I enjoyed the one on one sessions with my new student. She was a captive audience.

One evening after she attended a financial empowerment meeting with me, I was driving home and Viv began to ask about being filled with Holy Spirit and speaking in tongues. I answered her questions and filled her in on as much as I could while driving, with the promise to show her more from the scriptures as soon as we got to my home. I was excited and happy to share my knowledge of Holy Spirit. With the extensive teaching from my pastor on the subject over the years and the classes while attending ministry school, I had been well equipped. In addition I had been a personal ministries worker (counselor) at my church for eight years at the time, so I had a pretty solid background in the knowledge of ministering Holy Spirit .

Once at home sitting at my dining room table, I opened my bible and showed Viv the scriptures that directly related to the indwelling of Holy Spirit. She told me that she was ready to receive the gift. She repeated as I led her in prayer asking the Father to fill her. After praying I encouraged her to speak in her heavenly language. The language that flowed from her was not like that of a babe. It was more eloquent. She was like a child that night, even more so than I had observed before. Needless to say, I was thrilled. As she left, I walked her to the door. She got in her car and drove off waving almost frantically and grinning from ear to ear.

Over the next few months Viv confided more and more in me. Her personal life and past became an open book. She told me how her mother had always mistreated her, and yet she was spoiled by her dad. Her parents were never married and her mother detested her dad. She constantly talked about how her mother favored her two siblings, Don and Linda and gave them anything they ever wanted. They had a different father and Viv believed that her mother hated her, because she also hated her father. She was born and raised in the South Carolina, but ended up living in Los Angeles with her mother after a bout with cancer which had reduced her from weighing three hundred pounds to her present weight of 125 pounds. She showed me a photo which proved she wasn't fabricating this, at least not the weight part. Supposedly she tried several times to take her life. She listened as I ministered to her, "the fact that thousands of sperm cells fought to fertilize her mother's egg, but she was the one that made it." I told her that most importantly, "God is a God of purpose and He has a purpose for your life."

I have always been a softy for the underdog and in this instance I yielded to that character trait as opposed to following the leading of Holy Spirit. I would embrace the one that others turned away, but at the same time I had always been selective of whom I allowed into my bosom; into my inner circle if you will. Usually sob stories were just sob stories to me, but this time it had to do with the physical appearance of this person, her five-year-old child and her poor health.

Viv was kind of pitiful in a lot of ways. Not only was she sickly, but she always looked sad. She told me that she was forty-four years old, and although she looked older, she demonstrated the mentality of a fourteen-year-old. Her skin was blotchy and leather-like, and her hair was so brittle and thin that you could see her scalp. I had no knowledge of the autoimmune disease called alopecia at the time, but in retrospect, that would probably be the diagnosis. Her legs were covered with hair and when she wore tops without sleeves, you could not ignore the stretch marks and the sagging skin. Besides that, the hair under her arms was like a shaggy bush. When I asked her why she chose not to shave under her arms, her answer was, "I've never shaved because my mama told me that I didn't need to shave my legs or under my arms." As I took all of this in, my heart went out to this woman. She looked like a victim of years of multifaceted abuse and she was that character in a book that I had read or in a movie that I had seen.

She listened and was very receptive as I gave her advice on physical hygiene and the care of her hair, skin and nails. I would take her shopping for facial moisturizers, scrubs, toners and other enhancers. I encouraged her to stop using harsh soaps, especially on her face, and to only buy moisturizing shampoos and conditioners for her hair. I introduced her to a hair stylist that gave her a completely new look. She began to get treatments for her hair, which was very short, but the stylist was able to put a weave in with lots of volume in the top that shaped into a cute tapered style. I introduced her to healthy eating, and to taking supplements that would help her hair and skin. I went through my closet and gave her suits, dresses, and in short a brand new wardrobe. She got blessed BIG time because we also wore the same shoe size. Viv didn't have a decent coat or jacket, so I gave her one of each. She seemed very grateful and couldn't stop thanking me.

A lot was going on in my life at this particular time. I was getting busy with ministry. My siblings and I were planning a surprise celebration honoring our parent's fiftieth wedding anniversary, and I was orchestrating everything from Los Angeles. At the same time my best friend was recovering from a stroke and a few times a week I would help her husband out by keeping her at my home during the day. We were knee-deep in preparations for our acting school's annual walkathon fundraiser and our upcoming summer conservatory. To top it off, that, one of our assistant pastors and instructor in the School of Ministry asked if I would consider the position of T. A. for his Evangelism class. Well, of course that's what I lived for! Although my plate was full, how could I say "no" to this great opportunity? I told the pastor I would pray about it and let him know. My prayer was for wisdom and direction. I knew that this would mean leaving our summer conservatory during the busiest time and being gone for at least half of the day.

One Saturday morning Deirdre and I were in the office after our prayer time swapping ideas about the summer conservatory. The phone rang and the person on the other end was hysterical. I kept saying, "Hello", and the crying just got louder with unintelligible babbling. Deirdre was about to go down and start her class, but realizing that this was not a normal phone call, she waited to see what was going on. I finally recognized Viv's voice and after several unsuccessful attempts to calm her down, I told her to hang up, pull herself together and then call me back. Almost immediately she calmed down and told me that her dad had just dropped dead behind the wheel of his truck of an apparent heart attack. Her dad lived in South Carolina, and from the way she had talked about him I knew this was a devastating thing for her. I would just do my best to help her get through. The next couple of nights I was scheduled to work she was off, but she would come by and sit for part of my shift. She told me that she was preparing to go home and bury her father. She cried a lot about the family situation and said that she was not looking forward to facing her brothers and sisters. Apparently she had three half sisters and a half brother that were her father's children. This was a separate set of siblings who had a different mother. Her father had been married to this woman and she was deceased. Viv called her Louise and had been fond of her step mom, because she treated her as one of her own. It seemed that when Louise died the children unsuccessfully went after their dad for certain items belonging to their mother. When he wouldn't turn things over to them, they took him to court. She said this really hurt her dad and caused him to make some major changes in his estate. She went on to say that she would never forget the day that her dad picked her up and asked her to go for a ride with him. She said he took her out to dinner and while they ate he shared what her siblings had done and told her that he was placing her name on everything that he owned, and was determined not to leave his other children anything.

The night before Viv left for South Carolina, she called me for prayer. She sounded so lost and depressed, like she was down in a deep well. I could hardly hear her and repeatedly asked her to speak up. I prayed with her and encouraged her to keep her eyes on Jesus and to pray continually in her heavenly language for victory over that depression. She promised me that she would, although as we hung up, I felt like I had failed to reach her.

The next morning around nine a.m., she called and said that she was at the airport. She sounded like a different person. She was bright and cheery. She was laughing and thanking me for my prayers and for being her only support system. I could hear lots of noise in the background and the announcements of boarding flights. She assured me that she was fine and that she was going to take my advice to be strong, keep her chin up and allow no one to take advantage of her. I prayed with her for traveling mercies and that the angels of the Lord be encamped around and about her as she goes and as she returns without incident. As I hung up the phone I remember thinking, truly what a difference a day makes. My soul was so happy for this girl. I thought...prayer had indeed reeled her out of the deep pit that I envisioned her in just the night before.

I didn't hear from Viv for about a week, but when she called she seemed so excited about the outcome of things. The first thing that she said was how proud of her I would be. She told me that her bossy sister only made one attempt to take advantage of her, but when she spoke up for herself, they were all quite surprised and the most trouble that she had after that was bad attitudes. I congratulated her when she told me that instead of using money left to her to bury her dad, she stood her ground and told one of her sisters to bury him with the policy that she had on him. She bragged about the new person that she had become. She said that she was sick and tired of being a pushover, and wanted to make her dad proud of her. I must say that in retrospect, she didn't appear to have a lengthy bereavement. She bounced back rather quickly, but I didn't spend too much time wondering why. In fact I was somewhat relieved about it, because she had begun to demonstrate her clingy side, and as I stated before, I already had a full plate.

Viv began sharing more and more of her family dynamics with me. She would call me crying about how her mother was treating her. One night she called and I could hardly hear her. She said she was whispering, because her mother's bedroom was right next door and she didn't want her to know that she was on the phone. She explained to me that her mother had taken two thousand dollars from her. The money was under her mattress when her mother found it and told her that she needed to make the mortgage payment for the month and pay some other bills. My new found friend seemed so helpless and pathetic. I found myself being emotionally involved. I was upset with her for being such a pushover and angry with this woman who called herself a mother. I thought her controlling behavior was way overboard. I had only spoken to her mother once and she seemed pleasant enough, but Viv informed me that she was jealous of our relationship and warned her about trusting people in LA. She told me that her mother would constantly compare people in South Carolina to people in LA. All people in LA were fickle, materialistic and untrustworthy. Well, of course she didn't believe that because she had already met my daughter and me. When I told Viv of my decision not to call her at home again, she was upset and informed me that she pays the bills and I could call her at any time. After much dialogue I got her to see my side; simply respect for her mother's home.

A week or so later my friend called me crying and nearly hyperventilating. She asked me what she should do. Her mother had demanded $10,000.00 to be in her hand within five days, and added, "That's just a drop in the bucket for him." She told me that her father's estate had not been settled as yet and her mom was after everything that she had. In the next breath she vehemently stated, "I'm not giving her anything." Silently I was saying, "Yes!", but from what she had previously told me about this woman's character, I knew there might be trouble ahead. I didn't give her any advice. Instead I told her to pray about it and perhaps think about getting her own place. She agreed that it was a good idea to move on her own. She went on to share how she got paid bi-monthly and had been signing her whole check over to her mom. I could only shake my head. I could hardly believe what I was hearing, but it got increasingly worse over the months to come. She told me of an attorney in South Carolina whose first name was Frank. She said this man had been a good friend of her father's and of the family for years. He was handling the business of her dad's estate and would be in touch with her. I was seeing another side of Viv now. She spoke out against her mother calling her a greedy witch. She said her mom was really giving her a hard time. The latest was that she had papers drawn up naming herself as power of attorney over Viv, and was attempting to prove her incompetence. Viv vowed to defend her dad's property at any cost.

8.
Satan Sets It Up

Viv asked me one day if I would consider being her power of attorney. I was taken aback by her request because she and her sister, Lucille in New York seemed to have a good relationship. In fact, she talked to her frequently and would often have a funny story to tell about her sister. When I denied her request, she became upset. I told her that I just did not feel comfortable assuming that responsibility with all that was going on. She said that her family reunion was coming up shortly and she wanted everything in place and safely protected from her mother, siblings and all other relatives whom she believed would do anything to get their hands on what her dad had left her. She told me that her mom had great influence over the entire family and they would do whatever she said. The family reunion was to begin in the Pocono Mountains of Pennsylvania and would conclude in Augusta, Ga. She made the comment that all of her family was against her and if anything should happen to her on this trip, she just wanted to know that her little girl would be taken care of by someone who had her best interest at heart. She seemed genuinely concerned and eager to get her business in order before taking this trip. I continued to hold out, making all kinds of excuses to prevent getting entangled in her family's affairs. I told her that I was there to help in any other way, but that I thought this was asking a bit too much, too soon. I had only known Viv eight months. I suggested that she ask her sister Lucille to be power of attorney; however that suggestion was met with great objection. She told me that I did not understand. She went on to say that even though she talks to her sister, there was some jealousy there. She said that Lucille was a good actress and that she could see right through the act. She believed her sister was in touch with the others and that her pretense was a setup. I stood my ground, but Viv was relentless. I had never met anyone with such tenacity. She asked me nearly every day for the next three weeks if I would please reconsider. I finally said that I would think about it. She kept reminding me that the time was getting short and that we had to get a lawyer to draw up a "durable power of attorney." Finally she came to me two days before she was to leave with tears in her eyes telling me that I was the only one that she could count on, the only one who has been there for her. She begged me to say, "Yes" to being power of attorney. I called an attorney friend of mine and reluctantly I went with her to get the papers drawn up. She paid his fee of $350.00 for the preparation of the **Durable Power of Attorney** naming myself as first conservator nominee and my daughter, Deirdre as first alternate nominee, and from there we went to have it notarized. I was given two copies for safekeeping and Viv took one with her. I still had reservations because of how things were going in her life. It seemed that she had no privacy at home because she claimed her mother randomly rambled through her things. I thought... if this was going on before, then all the more now. I felt afraid for my friend, but I didn't know how to help her. Of course I often thought about reporting her situation to the police, but not without her consent. After asking her several times why she put up with this nonsense, I finally came to the conclusion that she was no different than any other abused woman. I knew that it would take some time to work with her and I believed that eventually her self-esteem would reach a level whereby she would say, "Enough", and break this cycle herself.

The night that she left for her family reunion, she didn't seem excited at all. Her mom was really giving her a hard time about signing a paper that she had drawn up by an attorney stating that she would have power of attorney over Viv because she was incompetent and incapable of making decisions.

I wanted to stay in touch with Viv while she was away, so I gave her a pre-paid calling card and told her to keep me abreast of things. She called me the day after they arrived in the Pocono Mountains and told me that the trip had been miserable and she did not want to be there. The second time that day, she called crying. She said her mother had come to her room, shoved some papers at her and demanded that she sign them. She said they were papers giving her mother power of attorney over all that belonged to her. She refused to sign them. The next day when she called she said that her uncle had held her while her mother beat her with a belt in front of her daughter and niece. This was like a wild movie... unbelievable! I was deeply concerned for her, especially with her health issues. Besides the diabetes, she told me that she had heart problems for much of her life. I felt so helpless, but prayer was all that I could do for her.

When I heard from her the following day, she asked me if I had heard from her attorney, adding that she had gotten in touch with him, told him the situation and given him my number. Of course I never heard from him, but each time she called she insisted that I should have heard from him by now. I talked to my friend about getting out of that situation. I asked if she didn't realize just how unhealthy it was, and told her that she had become enslaved to that situation. The next time she called me it was from a hospital in Georgia. Supposedly her mother, grandmother and uncle had harassed her. She said they tried again to force her to sign papers giving her mother power of attorney and declaring that she was incompetent. Her sugar was near 500 and the last thing she remembered before lapsing into a diabetic coma was grandma asking her mother not to hurt her. When she regained consciousness she was in a hospital bed with mother, grandma and uncle standing over her. She claimed the doctors saw the belt welts on her and inquired, but her mother spoke up with some bizarre explanation. The doctor gave her mother all of the medical reasons why Viv should remain hospitalized, but she wouldn't hear of it. She told him that with the trip ahead of them, it was too far to drive back and pick her up. She claimed that the doctor helped her get in touch with the attorney, who was angry about the situation, and told her to get to him and he would take care of everything. She gave me an address in Augusta, GA., and I wired her $125.00 so that she could take a bus to meet the attorney in South Carolina. I was getting perturbed at this point, but I had plenty to keep me busy. I was spending late nights at the studio since we were in the final stages of preparation for our summer conservatory.

After a week or so Viv returned home and so did the drama. She received a ticket for driving in the carpool lane of the freeway entrance and it was discovered that she had no insurance. Her story was that she had given her mom the insurance payment, but she had obviously spent it on something else. I admit, my antenna should have been way up, but again, I had my own life and plenty to keep me occupied. I was mainly there for moral support for my new found friend. The situation with the ticket ended up in court and Viv told me that the judge was charging her mother with her actions of spending the money that was given to her for insurance coverage. I half listened to the drama that followed, but because she seemed to be in such turmoil, I encouraged her to come and find peace in my home. I could not understand why she wouldn't let go of such a toxic situation, but I reached back and recalled some things that I had learned about women who are abused in various ways.. She usually doesn't know how to break the ties. Most times it is those on the outside looking in that can manage to be so objective and even judgemental at times.. Often she would call me crying to the point of hyperventilating. This was the case on the day that she called crying and sounding more pitiful than I had ever heard her. She informed me that her Uncles, Joe and Lonnie were helping her mother hold her captive in the house until she would agree to sign papers giving them power of attorney. I told her to call the police. She said she had called them and when she heard them at the door, her mother answered and deterred them by showing a document stating that Viv was mentally challenged. Now before this, she had shared with me that she tried to commit suicide at the age of twenty-one and was held in a mental facility and evaluated for 72 hours. She said that her mother never let her forget it and used that incident at every opportunity. I asked her where Babbi was during all of this and was told that she was at a neighbor's. Even after I invited her into my home and told her that she did not need to continue living like that, it took her awhile to make the actual move. And it was only after I finally told her not to call me again crying, and complaining if she was insistent upon staying there and taking the abuse. I was very firm, and she realized I meant business. When she made the move, I gave she and Babbi my extra bedroom and told her to feel at home.

Viv began sharing how she had made multiple trips to the hospital with Babbi because of her inability to have normal bowel movements. She told me the child would sit and cry for long periods of time while trying to go to the bathroom. Right away I asked about the child's diet. I found that she had been feeding her fast food for breakfast, lunch and most of the times, dinner. I told her that there was no wonder the child was constipated. Viv could not remember the last time the child had eaten fresh fruit or vegetables. She would buy fast food on the way to school each morning and because she worked at the same school that Babbi attended, she would take her out for more fast food at lunchtime. Dinner most nights was a repeat of this. I was livid. I could not believe that an educator was so oblivious of the obvious reasons that her child's system might be messed up.

I explained to Viv that I did not care to spend my time in hospital emergency rooms. She understood and agreed that we would need to do things differently now that they were with me. We would have home cooked and prepared meals. We would eliminate all fast foods from the child's diet. Babbi would have fruit and vegetables everyday. She would have a good breakfast each morning before school and we would pack a lunch each night complete with fruit.

9.
Reeled In

Things got off to a good start with my new house guests. Viv had gone to court several times now concerning the tickets that she received. Deirdre and I made sure that she could go and deal with the situation without being concerned about Babbi, who was now in our Summer Conservatory acting classes all day, everyday. We had taken this child under our wings and would make sure that everything was okay for her. Babbi was a natural in class; a little on the hyperactive side, but she had no inhibitions. We believed in discipline, so when she wouldn't listen, her punishment was to sit upstairs in the office with me. You could say it was my punishment too. She would fire away with question after question, so I never got very much done until she was allowed back into class.

By now I had said, "Yes" regarding the Teacher's Assistant position in the school of ministry. Of course I would work it out. This was a great opportunity! It was helpful that this was a summer school position. It would be a three hour class, once a week for six weeks, and would run concurrently with our summer conservatory. I was still working part-time nights at the mental health facility, but had encouraged Viv to resign when her disability kicked in. She appeared to be oblivious of the fact that she could get in trouble for working and drawing state disability at the same time.

It turned out that Viv presented one episode of drama after the other all summer long, but, I was too busy to get caught up in every little detail. No doubt, I wish I had paid more attention, but my style of helping people to stand on their own is one of hands off and sometimes tough love. By now the situation with her dad's estate was turning into a daily fiasco. The next thing I knew the judge, who ruled in her favor concerning the insurance that went unpaid by her mom, was now her protector from her mother and others who would later join the cast. She called him Judge Evans. She certainly had a way about her that made people want to take care of her. In retrospect, she manipulated her web so that she caught every potential prey. She was very good at what she did. The things that she told me about this woman whom she called "mother" totally convinced me that she was twin to the wicked witch of the north. I found out much later that the woman was not her mother, but an evangelist, who had fallen prey just like myself. According to Viv her "mother" was a "big wig" in the Church where they attended. She obviously was loved and respected by the people there, but Viv saw her as a socialite. She would call on Sundays after church to tell me how long she and Babbi had to sit in the car hungry and bored, and wait while she talked to what seemed like everyone in the church before they could go home.

One day she was sharing and crying about how this woman would take her pay check each week, deposit it into a joint account which they had together, then withdraw the money and spend it on her own pleasures. She claimed she was really tired of it and wanted to go to the Bishop of this church to report what she called the "facts." She appeared very angry and said she wanted to expose the "real Mother Craig" to the Bishop of the church. I thought: "Finally she's had enough and is willing to fight back!" I agreed to help draft a letter in her words. Being careful to allow her to tell the story, I agreed to correct grammatical errors and edit it.

In this letter she began by informing the bishop that she was forced to take a stand at this time because of the dynamics relative to her relationship with her mother. She went on to say that it began when her dad died three months prior. She wasn't at church during that time, because she chose to leave quietly to bury her dad and return without having to share the details of her loss. I remembered this detail specifically, because I asked why she would keep something of that nature from the people who could possibly help in this time of bereavement and need. She convinced me that I didn't know those people and that anything they gave her would end up in the hands of her mother, and she would never see it. That was explanation enough for me, and if that's the way she wanted it, I was in full support. In her words she wrote to the Bishop, "My dad was the most important and influential person in my life and I have not been given the opportunity to grieve or express my pain. Thanks to my mother (who was never married to my father), I am forced to feel like I'm on a battlefield, fighting for what is rightfully mine. Approximately two days after I returned to Los Angeles with the heaviness of my loss on my heart, my mother began harassing me. She demanded that I give her $10,000 within forty-eight hours. She despised my father and I knew that I was in for war, because at that very moment, I decided that I would not honor her request. Because I did not wish to prolong my stay once I buried my father, all of my business was left in the hands of a very capable family attorney until I could return to take care of it. Giving her $10,000. was out of the question.

I am diabetic, and an episode caused me to be hospitalized. Before going into the hospital I cashed my paycheck in the amount of $2,300. and placed the cash under my mattress. When my mother visited me in the hospital, her attitude was hostile. She threw two receipts on my bed and informed me that she had taken all of my money. She paid her property taxes, and then paid her car insurance with the balance. I was livid, but dared not show it. I just wanted to be left alone with memories of my father, but instead I was constantly being harassed and abused; mentally, emotionally, and physically by my mother.

On June 2, I received another paycheck in the amount of $2,000.00, plus a vacation check for $2,000.00 (totaling $4,000.00). My mother took the liberty to forge my signature on both checks and deposited them into her account. She went to my job and volunteered false information regarding my ability to function as a teacher. As a result of this, I was given a leave of absence without opportunity to plead my case. Within two weeks time my mother had gone through $6,000.00 of my money, wiping out all of my savings. Bishop, I love my mother very much, but found that her lust for money exposed some issues that I had been blinded to all of my life.

I realize that she never loved me. I am not speaking out of anger when I say this. It is a painful truth. I have spent all of my life trying to buy my mother's love. It took my father's passing to bring me to the place where I finally see my mother in her true light; greedy and relentless, stopping at nothing to destroy me. There is a string of incidents so numerous and painful for me that I choose not to rehash them. I will, however share this.

In May, my attorney sent rent checks from my father's income property in the amount of $5,000.00. I never saw the checks. I found out that the package arrived on Friday. My mother signed for it, opened it, forged my signature and once again, deposited them in her account. Something snapped inside of me. I had had enough! I called my attorney to inform him, and to let him know I was in need of my money, because I was without anything at all. I received counsel as to what I needed to do. On the following Monday morning my attorney called the bank and asked that they hold the checks until I arrived to verify the signature on them. My mother was asked to accompany me to the bank to verify that she both signed and deposited the checks without my knowledge or permission. She asked me numerous times to lie on her behalf, but I could not and would not do it. At the bank I verified that the signature was not mine. She had falsified information stating that I gave her permission to sign my name. Once at home, the torture began. She slapped me with all her might several times because I would not answer when she went on her rampage. Besides pulling my hair out from the root, she was also verbally abusive. She has placed a gun in my room to coerce me into taking my life. There was a time when I did not want to live and she remembers those times. Now, when depression comes and I feel like dying, I remember the scripture that was ministered to me. "Do not allow Satan to take your life. He is the thief, and he only comes to kill, steal and destroy."

My mother hired a lawyer with the money that she took from me to plant a case against me. He also tried to get me to cooperate and lie on her behalf. The case against me stated that I was mentally challenged and incompetent to the point that I needed her to handle all of my affairs and make all decisions on my behalf. She even went so far as to fabricate how medication had severely damaged my brain, and that the deterioration has caused me to become forgetful of what I have said. She told the officers at the bank that I gave her permission to sign my checks, but because of my condition I had forgotten. As a result of the forgery, the bank pressed charges and we ended up in court with my mother denying that she forged the checks and me refusing to lie about giving her permission. The entire abuse situation came out during that first court date, because the doctor who treated me for the bruises testified on my behalf. My mother was reprimanded and warned by the judge that if she ever abused me again, she would go to jail. My mother was determined to defy the law. She said that no one was going to tell her what to do. The very next day she took advantage of the fact that I was sick and very weak. She grabbed me with such force, pushed my head into the bed, and hit me with her fist repeatedly. Again she tried to force me to go with her to the bank and lie. I told her that God hates a lying tongue. This made her furious! I was always like putty in my mother's hands, allowing her to control my life. I was forced to lie, cheat, and connive so that she could maintain her lavish lifestyle. She used me to get monies from my dad (whom she despised), and this went on from the age of nine until even now. She is still attempting to get every penny that was his. When the scales were lifted from my eyes, I began to see that I was so hungry for my mother's love that I would do anything to win it. I am finally taking a stand, making a decision to stop being the doormat that I've been all of my life. It is a sobering reality that my mother's lust for money even outweighs her love for God, and I struggle to understand how my mother, and evangelist of the church can have such contempt in her heart for her own child?"

The income property was supposed to have been a trailer park that her dad owned. In fact she told me that the attorney, Frank, would be collecting rent for now and sending her a check each month. To make things look authentic she showed me a list of thirty-three tenants, complete with first and last names and their unit numbers. She also told me about three bank accounts that her father supposedly put in her name. They were all in South Carolina, but in two different cities. She said he did this to assure that his other children would be clueless. She would brag about how smart her dad was and how he had worked for one of the judges for years and invested every penny that he made.

10.
Cast of Many Faces

Over the next several months, a continual chain of events unfolded. One day at the top of our summer conservatory I was overwhelmed with new enrollees, phones ringing off the hook, an office full of parents with questions, etc. Right in the middle of all of this, Viv called to inform me that her mom had been arrested. I remember thinking; it's about time that arrogant bully got her just due. Growing up in the big city, I have known my share of female bullies. They could get anything they wanted; going to any lengths and taking any dare that came their way. They would lie, steal and manipulate without a conscience and never gave a care who got hurt in the process. No one wanted to challenge them, so they got away with it. Even when judgment befell them they never made the correlation. It was always unfair; someone else's fault or they were the real victims. This is the picture that Viv had painted of "Mother Craig". Consequently I had no compassion for this woman. She was free in no time, but arrested again about a month later after following Viv from a fast food drive thru to a prominent department store parking lot where she apparently pulled a gun on her and threatened to blow her brains out. The two guys with her mom were arrested too. However they told the judge they didn't know what was going on. The mom saw Viv's car and said, "That's my daughter, follow her"…and they did.

In addition to the money that I wired Viv when she was in Georgia, she continued to borrow with the promise to pay it back with interest after her dad's affairs were sorted out. I told her that interest would not be necessary, but she insisted, telling me what a blessing I had been to her and how she felt obligated to give back far more than she had received. She was upset with Frank because he was moving too slow and she reminded him that she had to borrow from me while waiting for him to get things in order. She needed money for car insurance, and for the title to her car, which she said was being transferred out of her mother's name. It was nearing September, and since she no longer had the teaching job, she was in search of another private school for Babbi. She talked about Babbi's hyperactive nature and how she did so much better in smaller classes where she was less stimulated. Deirdre and I happened to know the owner of a private school just across the street from our studio whose granddaughter had taken acting classes with us. We took Viv and Babbi over and introduced them. Of course she needed money for registration and the first half of tuition because her monies were "still tied up". We agreed to loan her the money, because the way things sounded we would have it back in a few weeks.

Soon afterwards Viv informed me of finding that her mom and Frank were in cahoots all along. Apparently he was the one who prepared the power of attorney that was being pushed at Viv by her mother. The plan was for Frank and mom to split the inheritance; Then Frank would keep all of her dad's equipment and mom would keep the contents of the house, which supposedly included lots of expensive antiques. She called him to let him know that he had been found out and that she was reporting him to the Bar Association. Now things would be at a standstill again until she found another attorney.

As soon as our summer classes were over I immediately got busy with the mass mailing of our newsletter and announcements of upcoming fall classes. I also picked up two additional ministry assignments through our Ministerial Assistance Program, and I was excited! Through this program, I would now receive my ministry license.

Viv and Judge Evans, as she called him, seemed to be really bonding. According to her, he despised crime and those who took advantage of others. He was going to see her through this nightmare. I'll have to be honest. I felt a great sense of relief because I would not have to get involved on a greater level. I figured he could do a far better job rescuing her from those that were "out to get her" than I could. The mere fact that he was a part of the justice system put me at ease in the situation. I thought the judge's involvement was a bit over-extended, but I was beginning to feel stretched to the point that I was happy to put my ideas and ideals aside and let him "go for it."

I had never heard Viv sing, but she often mentioned how she sang at church and at funerals. Apparently a church member, Mrs. Senter had died and she had been asked by the family to sing at the funeral the following Sunday. She had spoken of this lady from time to time. On Saturday night she called me at work to remind me that she was singing at the funeral the next day. She wanted to know if I thought it would be a good idea to let Babbi spend the night with a lady named Ms. Cook. Their daughters were the same age and the kids wouldn't be attending the funeral. I thought this was okay since the lady nor her family knew Viv's mom. However she later told me that she was followed, and once she dropped Babbi off and left, two Hispanic guys took her uncles, Lonnie and Joe, her sister, Brenda, and grandma to Ms. Cook's house. They threatened Ms. Cook and told her they knew the child was in there. Ms. Cook supposedly became frightened and opened her door not wanting any trouble. The conclusion was that they wanted to send a clear message to Viv that neither she nor Babbi were safe anywhere.

When I left work I felt led to drive a few blocks past the house, and then circle around before going in the back to park. As I came back down towards the house, I spotted a dead white kitten right by the side of Viv's tire on the driver's side of her car. She was petrified of cats, so I told her about it to prepare her before she saw it on Sunday morning. She told me she believed it was planted there.

Viv had decided to join my church. On the second Sunday in August she would attend her first day of the new member's class before she sang at the funeral. She looked nice in her black suit and I gave her pearl earrings with a matching pin to compliment her outfit. Later that evening she shared the events of the day. The first thing that she told me in a somewhat skeptical manner was that the pastor who taught new member's class came up to her and said, "Sister, I sense that you're going through something, and whatever it is, God is your strength. Here's my card, and if you need counseling, call the church office and make an appointment." I asked why she looked so spooked about it. Her answer was that she felt uneasy that he was able to "read her mail". I didn't realize that this was also a lie. I wasn't fully aware of the church's protocol policy in reference to pastoral counseling until much later when I was assigned to the prayer lines as a part of our Ministerial Assistant Program. In retrospect, the person in need of pastoral counseling always made the initial contact, not the pastor. So in my ignorance I assured her that only by the Spirit of God could this man know anything about her. I had great respect for him. He had been one of our assistant pastors for many years and had been one of my instructors in several classes when I attended the school of ministry. He was a scholar and a man of deep revelation knowledge, so what she said did not surprise me at all. She probably went to him after class with one of her sob stories, at which time he offered her his card. Part two of Viv's eventful day happened during the funeral while she was singing. She looked in the back of the church and saw her daughter sitting with Ms. Cook, and on the same row were her two uncles, her sister, and grandma. I am sure that I had seen something like this in the movies.

Viv's account of another day in court: Monday morning she went to see Judge Evans and had this to say, "My two uncles along with my sister, grandma, Mr. Cal and friends, plus the two Hispanic fellows were brought in for questioning today. When the judge told them that they could either start talking or they would all go to jail, Uncle Lonnie told everything. He said that my mom had promised them $20,000 each to help her get me out of the way. He also exposed that mom had been mixing up potions for me to drink, and how she had put stuff in my food, but I wouldn't eat or drink anything that she made. Uncle Lonnie told her that he and Joe couldn't participate in killing me. Orders were given by my mother to give me a heart attack by planting the cat next to my car. Uncle Joe had killed the cat, and the Hispanic guys told Judge Evans that they were instructed to plant the cat. Uncle Joe got thirty days in jail, and grandma was warned that she would be next. The Hispanic guys got community service. Uncle Lonnie also said that Frank came with them to LA, and stayed for three days." A few days later Frank tried to commit suicide according to Judge Evans. He was hospitalized with 24-hour surveillance. Judge Lee, whom Viv's dad was supposedly employed with for years called from South Carolina to give Judge Evans this news. Apparently Frank received the letter from the Bar Association and became unglued.

While in the midst of preparing for production and participating in community related events with our kids, rest assured that Viv's drama never ceased. We were packing up and loading our cars after a community fair on the church grounds when we discovered that Viv had a flat tire. I called roadside service, but the guy found it impossible to remove the tire. He said the lugs were stripped. Air was put in the tire so that it could be driven to the closest tire shop. Viv was able to find a place nearby. She came back with another story that a detective, (apparently dispatched by Judge Evans) followed and stopped her to let her know there had been more arrests.

The next day was busy. In the midst of wrapping up our final day of production, everything that could go wrong did! We were supposed to gain entry to the theatre at 10:00 a.m. Parents had dropped their kids off early and wouldn't return until the 3:00 p.m. performance. Wouldn't you know it? Somewhere there was a breakdown in communication and we couldn't get into the theatre until 1:00 p.m. Thank God for the faithful ones. We had about five parents, who stuck around to help us transport 50 kids back to our studio just in time to feed them lunch at noon and get back to do the show on time. Right in the midst of trying to coordinate things Viv called to report another close call wherein her assailants were immediately apprehended.

Needless to say, my days were quite productive when Viv was not around. She supposedly had to be in court at 10 a.m. the next morning.

With a "to do" list a block long, I kept Babbi for her and took her on all of my runs. The list of performers and participants in Viv's production just kept growing. That evening she rattled off the following scenario... "Judge Evans called the whole slew in! My mom, sister, Uncle Lonnie, two Hispanic brothers who followed me and their two cousins; Akim (a former border of her mom's, who was hired to find a hit man); Mother Goudeaux, Sister Shaeffer, Morgan, and three Black guys hired by Akim as hit men. Judge told my mom that he was recommending stiff sentencing for her after learning from all that she tried to coerce each of them into taking Viv's life. He said the potions that she had been concocting had all of them acting as though they had no brains. Mother Goudeaux was the sanest. She spoke on my behalf that she had never seen a young lady love her mother so much.

The following day Viv reminded me of a purring kitten as she pranced around recalling the courtroom saga of the day. More of Mother Craig's cohorts were given sentences and she blurted out that she hated the day Viv was born. In her words, "They all piggybacked on each other's statements that I had always been trouble to my mother. My sister from Georgia was arrested after being found with over $2,000.00 at the home of the Hispanic family. She broke down in court and said that she would go to her grave doing whatever my mom asks her to do. I was not enthused when Viv told me that the Judge had appointed a therapist for her, in fact I was a bit troubled. It's a personal thing going back to my days in mental health. For over nine years I had various opportunities to minister to people who were mentally challenged, but had a desire to get well. Sometimes they were already saved, but would seek me out to talk about prayer, and ask what they needed to do to be strong and stay focused. They would express a desire to be free of psychotropic drugs. I always gave scripture that would coincide with whatever they were going through, but many times my intervention was circumvented by encouragement to remain on the drugs. I realize that many could not stay focused or even be productive without the medication; however, it was disturbing to watch some of the judgment calls to increase or add medication that simply was not in the best interest of the patient. Things had shifted from what was once about the welfare of people to being about filling beds and increasing revenue. It had become a lucrative business and frankly, a conflict of interest.

After Viv's first session, she told me that the therapist wanted to hypnotize her. She had enough sense to say, "Absolutely not!" She said the therapist, broke out the tarot cards and followed by reading Psalm 1:38 from the bible. Really!?.. I thought.

Deirdre called on Saturday and wanted us to spend some time together. I felt like going to the garment district, and invited Viv and Babbi to come along. As we dodged around the crowds enjoying the sights, Viv appeared withdrawn and said several times that she should have stayed at home. I convinced her that she had made the right decision to get out. We had a good time; shopped a little, ate and headed back in time for Deirdre to go to work. Viv was scheduled for therapy, but did not want to go. She waited until the last minute and then went on. Of course I kept Babbi and took her to the store for some dessert. When we returned, Viv was sitting in the living room withdrawn and quiet. As I headed towards the kitchen, she blurted out, "She struck again. When I left the therapist, two Black guys were waiting in a car and shot at me. I wasn't hit, but they hit a car in front of mine. Wayne (the detective) got them immediately and called for back up. They were arrested and Judge Evans was notified." She appeared really shook up over this one. After hearing the gunshots, Viv said the therapist immediately ran out to see if she was ok. I remember thinking.... "That is strange and fishy." Usually when there's gunfire people take cover. No one runs out!

The next day Viv was still shook up, and wanted to stay in all day. I decided to get her out of the house. Her car was now "marked", so it was unsafe to drive. I took her to my favorite mall in Glendale and we stayed until it was time for me to go to work. She kept my car and was to pick me up at midnight. At 9 p.m. she called and asked if she could bring my car to me, because she was "feeling like doing something." I asked what she was talking about and she repeated herself. I told her that she was talking crazy and being selfish; that too many people had put themselves out to help her. I got busy and had to hang up, but called her back and told her to come to my job and stay with me until I get off. Viv arrived within 30 minutes. She was upset with me and said I owed her an apology for yelling. She couldn't understand what she had done wrong. After we talked about it and I explained how I had invested in her; my heart, time, prayers, etc., she finally understood and we both apologized.

The following day Viv went to the hospital because of persistent chest pains. She insisted on driving herself, but returned around mid afternoon to check on her daughter and didn't seem to want to talk about her hospital visit. After much probing, she admitted that they wanted to keep her and monitor her heart, but she left the hospital. After a pow-wow between us she agreed to lie down for a couple of hours and then go back. After returning to the hospital she called to say that she was admitted, and wanted to talk. I calmly reminded her of my schedule and of the fact that I needed to prepare her daughter for bed. I was running out of gas, but I knew that it would soon be over, so I would push myself to endure. Viv came out of the hospital doing fine and resumed her court appearances. One afternoon she called crying and very upset, saying that she had to make some tough decisions. Her mother had hired more suspects to take her life. She even named two people from her former job at the residential facility. Judge Evans recommended that she divorce her family and make the decision now not to have anything to do with any of them ever again. She wanted to be sure that we (Dee and I) were really going to be her family because this would be a drastic move. I thought, "Have I been watching too much TV, or what?" This was getting somewhat nerve wracking and at the same time, it was intriguing. I knew that one-day I would have to tell this story. I just had no idea that I would be the real victim. According to Viv her Aunt Ruellen and Uncle Bill showed up from Georgia. Her aunt was furious with her for not coming to her and telling about this charade. Her aunt offered her and Babbi a home with her, but Viv said, "No". She said that her mother had the audacity to ask her if she could talk with her before she makes any decisions, and her aunt begged her not to be hasty, but to pray about it.

11.

Mega Drama

Viv managed to get an appointment to counsel with one of the assistant pastors. She came home ecstatic, talking about what the Lord showed him about her situation. She very cleverly shared the details of the session, using a **Word of Knowledge** as a decoy to make this story sound authentic. Truth of the matter is…it worked. These are the words that flowed from her mouth…"I was shocked that Pastor was so accurate concerning everything that was going on with me. Through him, God said that nothing is going to happen to me because my angels are all around me; when I walk out of the door, when I'm driving in my car, and when I return, I am always protected. God also revealed to Pastor that he was looking at an extremely wealthy woman and although my funds have been tied up, it won't be long before I will have it all in my hands." And Pastor spoke very highly of you and told me to accept the new family that God had given me. I told him that there were things that I didn't want him to know, but God had already showed him everything to prove to me that He is real, He's got my back, and wants me to know that all is well. My new family is in tact, so I'm not to worry that things will change or that anyone would betray me. He encouraged me to be joyful right now, and act as though my funds are in my hands. Pastor even saw me challenged with diabetes and told me that God is healing me and that the doctor would soon say, "You no longer have diabetes." Of course I was excited for her, and was convinced that God was using me to influence two special little lives. Viv would say repeatedly, "I would be dead by now if God had not put you in my life when He did." From the looks of her life, I believed that.

Keen discernment is so important. Being filled with Holy Spirit is wonderful and needful, but He only prompts us and gives us an unction (that we should either back off or go forward), but He does not and will not control our choices. If we do not listen to the One who shows us things to come **(John 16:13)** it could be disastrous for us. There are people whom Satan has dispatched and assigned to cut off your ministry in its infancy, and to abort the plan of God for your life. Viv without a doubt was the diabolical instrument set up as an ambush to thwart the plan of God for my life and my ministry. A movie that I once saw called; "Sleeping with the Enemy" came to mind. A wolf in sheep's clothing was sleeping under my roof every night for a whole year and I chose to think that I was sent to be her savior.

Sometimes when we have a heart of compassion for hurting people we can get over into spiritual pride and we aren't even aware of it. We can run right over the voice of God with the "vacuum cleaner of life", as my pastor has so often said. I recalled a statement that was made when I first got saved. Someone told me that "everything that's good ain't God." Puzzled, I asked what they meant by that. They answered, "Just because you step out to do what seems like good, does not always mean that it is God telling you to do it. Perhaps it is for someone else, or on the other hand, it could be a set-up for your demise" …as in my case.

Back at the courthouse, Aunt Ruellen took the stand and told everything concerning Viv's childhood and how her mom treated her. Her siblings got the royal treatment while she was the underdog. She told how the mother extorted money through Viv from her father. Her dad would give her large sums of money while she was in college and she would hand it over to her mom. She had to wash, cook, clean, etc., but her siblings had no responsibilities. She said that Viv always tried to buy her mother's love and would shower her with expensive gifts. She claimed that her aunt broke down several times, and blamed the mother for making it impossible for Viv to trust any of the family. She personally wanted to meet and thank me, "the person who helped to keep her niece alive." That never happened, because Viv claimed to be very skeptical and stated that she did not want her aunt to meet me. She asked Viv to call her that night because she was scheduled to return to Georgia in a few days. I encouraged her to call and show appreciation to her aunt for speaking up on her behalf and to let her know that she does not blame her for anything that has happened. I remember thinking, she's one of the few who didn't end up in jail. Viv really poured out the tears that night. She told me that she was so tired of her mother and even more tired of fighting. She felt like putting a knife in her stomach and not stopping. I comforted her as best I could, reminding her that God was still on the throne and Jesus remains Lord, even over this tiresome situation. As we were about to retire for the night, she hugged me and told me that she loved me very much. I reminded her not to be moved by what she hears. I told her that I could be walking in fear by all of the things I had heard thus far, but I refuse to be intimidated by a "snaggle-toothed" bully like Satan. That got a roar out of her. It was good to see her laugh for a change. She told me that I was comical and I told her that God has a sense of humor. I reminded her of the scriptures that, "A merry heart does good like medicine" and "The joy of the Lord is our strength."

Walking five miles a day, 5 days a week at the park or the beach was the norm for me. Viv having never walked as a means of exercise decided to give it a try. I encouraged her to do as much as she could and not to be intimidated if she had to stop a few times. She moaned and groaned all the way, but she made it. Later that day she was scheduled to go to a bank which was a good distance from where I lived in LA. She was to retrieve her funds of $100,000.00 that her mom had placed in an account with the pretense that Viv was terminally and mentally ill. I was extremely hopeful. I was sure that this was the end of my babysitting the emotions of this woman. She would get her money! It was enough to pay us back, get her own place, and be on her merry way. I would still be a friend, but there would be extreme limits and boundaries.

As Viv was leaving for the bank, she called Wayne (detective) to say that she was on her way out. He informed her that her mother, although in solitaire confinement, had managed to recruit someone to make phone calls and mail letters. She had been busted that morning for trying to sneak three letters out to hit men with instructions to get rid of Viv and she would pay them $10,000 each.

After arriving at the bank, Viv claimed to have found that Frank had sent her mother a Power of Attorney document along with the $100,000 check that belonged to her. She told the bank officer who she was and presented all of her ID, including her birth certificate, only to be told that Mrs. Craig had done business with them for a long time and was highly respected. When Viv informed them of her mom's present situation connected with forgery and fraud she said they did not believe her. She invited them to call the other financial institution to verify the matter. When she threatened to take them to court to get her money, they intimidated her with information of the legalities that would have to take place before anything could be released to her.

Back at court that day, the fiasco continued and she was able to find out who the three culprits were that the letters were sent to. When I look back at my journal I am amazed at my deep compassion for this charade of lies.

Entry: "The fiasco never ends. My God! Viv said that her Aunt Ruellen had been at court all day waiting to see and talk to her. She asked Viv to allow her to be a part of her life, since she wasn't a part of the charade. She didn't give her aunt an answer, but told me an emphatic, "No!" She doesn't want to deal with any more "snakes." I am glad that she can trust me, and it's so good to be there for her at this time. This has been like the Twilight Zone."

Another trick of the enemy is using a person who paints everything as a deep dark secret. You alone are privy to this top secret information. I was deceived thinking that her confidence was solely in me to keep her secrets. No one else could be trusted.

Viv had mastered this and she used it to the max.

Many nights I witnessed this women self-administering insulin which she kept in the fridge. Sometimes the monitor would read 375 and up to 425 for her sugar level. A few times after a so-called heavy day in court, she would complain of chest pains and take a small pill under her tongue that she said was nitroglycerin. I had been to the hospital with her and brought her personal belongings home when she had to stay for a few days. When I picked her up to come home, the nurse gave her a new kit for the insulin with a fresh supply of the medication and strict instructions to watch her sugar levels. Even though she could not fake this she often resorted to using her poor health to continue weaving the web of deception, and she had a way of making things look authentic. Case in point… one day as I was leaving my post on the prayer lines, the receptionist who happened to be my good friend answered a call. It was Viv calling for an appointment. When I heard my friend repeat her name, I gave her a message that I was on my way home. Again, in retrospect, I realize that she knew I was in the pastoral department at that time. She also knew that my friend was answering phones close by.

She was making sure that I knew she was trying to continue with counseling and checking my whereabouts at the same time.

While all of this was going on my very close friend and wife of my mentor, (Pastor J.) was sick. Many times I would have to fly to Vegas to be with her when he had to minister out of town. It was unnerving how Viv seemed to be even more needy when I was away. She would call just as I was bathing or feeding my friend. I would tell her that I would call her back, but she would call again within a short period, posing the question, "Do you have time to talk to me yet?" Once when this happened I decided to talk to her the second time she called. She could not wait to flood me with the drama about how she had spent most of the day before in the hospital. She told the wild tale that the judge allowed her to go to the house along with Wayne (the detective) and her mother to search for money that had been stashed. Wayne went off into the attic leaving the two women alone. She was called into her mom's room and told that she had two weeks to call off everything, or there would be no more threats on her life…she would be a corpse. She claimed that she was warned not to mention this, however she thought it would be "deceiving" not to tell me. I told her that not only did I need to know, but the judge needed to know as well. It made me furious to know that the detective was so dumb. This all had to be coming to an end real soon! I was not ready for the next piece of news, but if the truth were told I felt a sense of relief.

12.
Suckered

The day had been long and exhausting. After Deirdre and I conducted the orientation for our upcoming winter session I went straight to a wedding, then on to work until midnight. Viv called me at work to report the traffic observed going in and out of her mother's house. This time four white guys were involved and the judge didn't like it. He now wants to put her in protective custody until he finds out what is going on. He supposedly had a lead that he would be following up on.

This of course meant that I would be taking care of this little girl while her mother was away. Simply put, I fell for it. She would be gone from the end of September until mid-December. It just seemed like the lesser of two evils to have Viv at a distance for awhile. My patience was running out. It seemed that no matter where I was, whether at work, at the studio, or on a ministry assignment, she always needed to find me and there was always a crisis. At one time I noticed a pattern particularly when I began to prepare for a ministry assignment. I would be dressing and without fail she would knock on my door and ask if she could talk to me. When it persisted I stopped her one day and firmly told her that I would appreciate her consideration when I am preparing to minister. I brought to her attention the times that she found reason to interrupt my preparation with what I called foolishness. She actually apologized and after thinking about it for a moment, told me that I was right and that she would never do that again. I honestly was not prepared for that smooth exchange. However, she kept her word and it never happened again.

When I read my journals that chronicle this story my emotions would go on a roller coaster ride. The trail of lies and deception were extended to such great and incredible lengths. Taking on the responsibility of a hyperactive six-year-old was not in my plans, but saw it as another opportunity to minister. All of my heart desired for Viv to be victorious over the situation that had seemingly engulfed her. If I could in any way be instrumental in helping her take control of her life and be a role model for her child, then my reaching out would not be in vain.

The drama unfolded right into the Sunday morning that Viv was leaving to go into "protective custody." She explained that she would be staying at the home of a detective (Jerry) and his wife. He would be assigned to escort her to court and the likes. I suggested that we have prayer, and afterwards she wanted to wait outside for the cab that was to pick her up. When she sensed my suspicion, she decided to wait inside. After I went into my room to get dressed for church, I heard her yell something that I couldn't understand. Quickly she was out the door and out of sight. She later told me that she had gotten her mother's sister-in-law to pick her up in her mother's car. The car was taken without permission and when the judge found out; he demanded that she take the car back, and she was also to inform me of what she had done. This was staged to look like a rebellious act for having to go into protective custody. Her excuse was that she was only taking what belonged to her. She mentioned several times that she was making the car payments.

With Viv in "protective custody", my days were full to the max and she seemed more desperate and needy. She could be so inconsiderate and self-centered, often calling two and three times a night. Sometimes Babbi and I were just getting in and she would want to talk. I would give Babbi the phone while I was getting settled, but after a few minutes she would desperately need to tell me about the events of the day. If I asked her to call back a little later, she would get offended. I was firm in sticking to a schedule because I needed to have Babbi in bed early, so that she would have ample sleep and I would have an easier time getting her up.

I changed my prayer time to an hour earlier. I would get her in the bathroom, dress and feed her, then take her to school. After picking her up from school, we might run errands and then it was home to start dinner. I was saved from doing homework because the children were helped with it after school. Babbi had to be scrubbed down every night. She played hard…as if she would never play again. She wore a uniform to school and the white shirt and socks were always black. She was a busy body and a talker in class, so I would have to attend extra teacher's meetings concerning her behavior. Nevertheless, the child was tugging at my heartstrings. She often seemed pre-occupied and easily distracted. She was certainly feeling the pulse of this whole charade. Insecure and having some separation anxiety, she had also become very clutchy. She was happy when I told her that her mom would be coming home on the weekends. After a few weeks Viv claimed that the judge had given her permission to spend some time with Babbi. This was a blessing in one way, and disruptive in another. Being much like a child herself, I found that I really had to adjust my rhythm to keep in sync. She would sometimes come home around mid-morning on Saturdays, and go back early Sunday mornings. Except for summer, our classes were from 9 – 5 every Saturday. Since Deirdre and I met early for prayer, I would have to get the child up and take her to the studio. Then once Viv was at the house, usually around 10:30, she would call and I would take Babbi to her and come back to the studio.

When I think of the Academy Awards, Viv concurrently comes to mind. I remember the first Sunday that she spent at home since being in "protective custody." I was preparing for church and putting last minute items together for a board meeting at the studio afterwards. She looked so pitiful, so sad. Her entire physiognomy read, "Please, let me stay here. I don't want to go back."

After church that day we were engaged in one of our most productive board meetings when the phone rang. Initially I thought it was one of our members calling to say they were on the way. Deirdre answered and handed the phone to me saying it was an emergency. Viv was on the line crying hysterically and telling me that she had been shot at again. The shots had come from two different directions. She was talking so loud that she could be heard across the room. I discretely asked her to pull herself together. I remember being frustrated at the time, that I couldn't say or do anything to help her. After hearing that the detective was with her and under cover cops nearby, I told her to call me later. Her story was that four gang members (Crypts) hired by her mom were arrested. The judge ordered that she be taken to the hospital and checked out. Her sugar and blood pressure levels were elevated. She seemed very angry and I listened while she vented. I empathized with her and told her that she had every right to be angry and frustrated with all of the madness. All she would talk about was coming home. I wondered to what lengths this would be taken for the love of money. Crypts!!? What's next? I could not imagine.

I was livid when I talked to Viv again. The following night she called me from the hospital. It seemed that so many slack decisions were being made concerning her safety. Her story was that after we talked, the detective took her to get a bite to eat, and in the interim she passed out and was taken to the hospital. After court the next day, she had another episode and her doctor was called.

The judge wanted her car so that he could set a trap for the gang members. The detective had Viv drive the "marked" car and he followed her to the doctor's, and then took off. After seeing the doctor, she called me to say that she came out and her car was gone. Immediately I knew that the car had been towed.

I found myself in a tizzy over the fact that not only was the detective careless, but Viv wasn't using her noodle concerning her own safety. She reported that the judge was beside himself concerning Jerry's decision to follow her in that car instead of calling him and waiting for further instructions. Viv said to me, "The judge has decided to move me to another location, and wants you to be involved in making the decision." She carried on about having to get used to another place. She just wanted to come home. That was understandable, but the reality was that she didn't have the capacity to be objective in the situation. She saw the judge as being unkind when he told her that she was not in position to make any decisions at the time. While I was sensitive to her wish not to be uprooted, my concern for what was best far outweighed my empathy.

I demanded to speak with the judge even though I had not planned to have any communication with him. I did not want my name documented in conjunction with this charade; however I was very upset and quite willing to let the record show that we had conversed. When Viv saw that I meant business, she went into her anxiety act which did not move me this time. She said that she would call the judge although she did not want to. She was ashamed that the record would show that she had used such poor judgment. I let her know that I was fed up with the nonsense! Now the car had been towed, another added expense to the many we already had. Amazing! We can be so blind and think that a matter is of God. I was deceived into thinking that it was God who placed me in this woman's life to help her. The enemy continued to use her to set trap after trap. It is only because of the grace and mercy of El Elyon, my most High God that I was not consumed.

When Viv asked if I was in agreement with the judge's decision to move her, I said I would give her an answer later. She was like a sulking child. She murmured and complained that no one understood and everyone was against her. Then she did something that some kids do when they want to make a good impression or when they want a "Yes" from a parent. While I was at work, she cleaned the house, did all of the laundry, ironed all of Babbi's uniforms, play clothes, and dress clothes for the upcoming week, plus helped her study and learn all of her spelling words for a test. When I came in from work she showed me all that she had done, then looked at me with a question on her face that asked: "Do I still have to go?" I gave her my answer, and she was not happy. She thought above all people that I should understand. I told her that her well being was more important than what she wanted right then. She accused the judge of treating her like a yo-yo. I told her that she was being ungrateful and that it would help if she tried to have a little insight concerning this. I reminded her of our commitment to teamwork. I cried out that night: "How long, O

Lord?" I was getting burned out with the constant battle with Viv over her own safety and well being.

More supposed family members joined the circus. The half sister and brother from New York, Lucille and Jerry showed up at court. An uncle Robert and his wife Frances came in from Georgia. Half sisters Danine, Corina and Nynah came in from South Carolina and brought Warren, an ex-boyfriend of Viv's with them. He had asked Viv to marry him some years ago, but it never happened. Now, he had invited himself to come and rescue her. She claimed that the sisters from South Carolina passed a letter in court begging her to meet with them for dinner so that they could talk with her one on one without intervention from the judge. She saw that as a trick and brought up the fact that if they turned on their own father, they would do the same or worse to her. Viv said they all blamed me for keeping her away from them. Upset because of Viv's decision to be estranged, Aunt Ruellen lost it in court and had to be restrained as she made threats against Viv. As the story progresses, Mother Craig's home was under surveillance, 24/7 and there were ongoing reports about the constant traffic. The home next door belonged to a woman named Connie whom Viv called her friend and she too was being watched.

The following week there was a problem with receiving her mail.

Although Viv changed her address a few months before so that her mail would come to my P.O. box, she was still having a challenge getting mail. I was with her when she put the change of address in at the post office, but each time I picked up mail there was none for her. I remember thinking that this was par for the course. It was all a part of the drama that was in progress. I was hopeful each time I went to get mail, but the story was the same; no mail for Viv. She always had a disgusted look on her face because she was expecting her checks from Babbi's dad in Texas, and her disability check. Finally she filed a complaint. After nearly three weeks and no satisfaction, she requested an investigation from the postmaster. Eventually the post office personnel end up in her web as a part of this on-growing cast. According to Viv, at least two postal workers were arrested after admitting to being hired to reverse the change of address.

Now, among the things that transpired in court:

Grandma and brother, Jerry were at each other's throats. After grandma testified that Jerry took money and a check belonging to Viv, Jerry lashed out at grandma in retaliation, accusing her of being behind all of the dirt dished out towards Viv. Uncle Robert's wife Frances was brought back in from Georgia and testified against her husband, saying that he got in touch with her the month before and told her to bring money. The gang members were given her number in Georgia and had been in touch with her as to how to make their moves. The gangsters told the court that Frances actually did the negotiating with them. The agreement was that they get the job done within a certain time frame, or they would not get the balance of their money. A strange guy came into the courtroom wearing dark glasses and a trench coat... Typical, right? When security checked him out, he had a gun. Again I thought, "Par for the course." The guy got past the device that was supposed to detect his gun and five hundred dollars cash was found on him.

The judge told Viv's sisters from South Carolina and Warren that they would not be able to come back to the courtroom. They had given Viv notes asking her to talk to them and the judge said, "No!" Warren gave Mother Craig a piece of his mind and Aunt Ruellen had to be escorted out again after threatening Warren for disrespecting her sister. This was a bit strange but not totally, considering that family members can be at odds with each other, but when an outsider attacks they come together.

After court Viv had an appointment to have her sugar level checked. She was escorted by Russell, (a retired detective appointed by the judge). The story goes that as they were exiting the elevator and headed for the car, Warren came out of nowhere, grabbed her arm and insisted on talking with her. When Russell called for help, four cops showed up and tried to take Warren down after he became unreasonable. He was so out of control that they had a tough time restraining him. He was taken to a psyche ward and placed on a 72-hr. hold.

Viv suspected that her sisters hired the guy with the gun and later told me that her suspicions were confirmed. The guy identified Corina as the one who approached him, and asked if he wanted to make some money. The sisters were arrested. When I asked Viv which one would initiate such a wicked act, she believed it to be Danine, because she was the eldest sister. It turned out to be Corina, but the shocker was that Lucille, (the sister in New York) engineered the set-up. The instructions to hire the man came from her, and they all let it be known the minute they got caught. Lucille was the sister that I thought Viv could trust. That was the reason that I denied her when she begged me to become her power of attorney. She talked about this sister all of the time, and spoke with her several times a week. She often told me how Lucille thought I was such a positive influence in her life. She wanted me to meet this sister, whom she seemed so close to. However, I remembered how she responded (almost in anger) when I suggested that she make Lucille "power of attorney." I thought it strange. She told me that I did not understand and that she didn't trust Lucille like that. This new information was a real shock to me.

Viv's brother in-laws came in from South Carolina to bail their wives out, but were told by the judge that they had wasted a trip. Corina's husband (a pastor) pleaded her case, claiming that her character and integrity were without flaw. The judge reminded him that she, (the first lady of their church) was guilty of hiring and paying a potential hit man. Nynah's husband claimed his wife's innocence, but was told that she was an accessory. Danine's husband did not come. The judge made a decision to move Viv once again. This time she was okay with the decision.

Now in her new environment, Viv called to tell me that she was not comfortable.

She claimed the detective that she had been placed with and his wife harassed her about the amount of her estate. I found this difficult to believe, unless these people were super arrogant or just plain stupid. I could not imagine that they would place themselves in a position that could get them fired immediately or have charges brought against them. The detective asked, "So, how much money are they trying to kill you for?" She said that his wife chimed in to say that, "He needs to know what he was putting his life on the line for." I suggested that she inform the judge immediately. After court the next day, she would have the uncomfortable experience of going back to the detective's home to get her belongings, and wait there to be escorted to appropriate placement.

13.
Precisioned Deception

The next morning I was just finishing prayer and about to get ready for church when Viv called crying hysterically. She told me that Warren had died that morning. For some reason this did not move me. I got a check in my spirit and thought…"More drama." I'm sure she felt the chill in the air. I was cool and unconcerned, but by this time I truly did not care. I talked with her for a few minutes and assured her that this was not her fault. She claimed that "everyone" was blaming her because Warren was calling her name before he died. I asked who was she referring to as "everyone" and she could not tell me. My response was "You are obviously blaming yourself since you can't tell me who "everyone" is." I told her that I was sorry, but I had no tears for the man, and I excused myself to get ready for church. I was relieved that she was coming by to take Babbi to another church with her this morning. More than ever I really needed my space.

That evening after Babbi was in bed, Viv told me that the judge had taken them out to eat and had complimented Babbi on her good manners. That was a plus because the child still had a long way to go. You are probably saying, "Gosh, you really believed that the judge went out to eat with a defendant and her child? Boy, you really fell for the okie-doke." Well, yes…and no. I made a choice. By now I was tired and I chose to tune out. My plate was overflowing. I didn't care what they did or what it took to bring this thing to a halt. I could have been inquisitive and engaged her with all kinds of questions. I certainly did have some. Sure, I thought it strange, but then I thought, "So what?" I just wanted my life and what belonged to us back. We know that everyone in the justice system aren't bad eggs, but there are enough of them that have their own agendas and those agendas are approved, overlooked, overshadowed and too often no action is taken against unethical conduct and practices. I was not about to become even more entangled. This woman had put the package of deception together like I have never seen it done. I remember asking her during a phone conversation what Warren's full name was. She seemed reluctant to tell me. Another check in my spirit! This made me quite curious. I asked what the big deal was about telling me his name. She kept skirting the issue and being evasive. I ended the conversation and hung up. She knew that things were coming to a head.

My upcoming week would be extremely busy with ministry assignments, work, running errands for the acting studio, and caring for Babbi.

I had finished helping Babbi prepare for a spelling test and we were having dinner when I received some very disturbing news. I congratulated her on her manners when she went to dinner with her mom and the judge. The child had a quizzical look on her face, and I realized that she didn't have a clue what I was talking about. She said, "No man went with us, only "Me, mommy and grandma." With as much composure as I could muster, I asked, "Grandma?" She said, "Yes, Grandma Bea," which was obviously her first name. I asked if grandma took them to church. She replied, "No, Aunt Millie picked us up on the street. We walked around the corner to that big street (which was LaBrae), and she picked us up and took us to our old church." Millie was a roomer at Mother Craig's. I asked if she had a good time, and with a wide smile she said, "Yes." She was excited about seeing her friends and said, "Grandma brought me and mommy back to her house, and then mommy and grandma stayed inside while I went outside and played with my friends."

I needed to sleep on this information. This was too much to digest at once. I felt like I had been sliced with a dagger. Wow! I was beside myself. I decided not to confront Viv as yet, but to do some investigating first. I made up my mind that the following Sunday after my church service, I would drive over to the Church where she claimed her mother was a member. I knew from previous conversations that they dismissed much later than our church, so I would have plenty of time to get there.

Although I had lots to keep me occupied, it seemed like the longest week of my life. Sunday finally came! Sitting in church, my mind raced and wandered throughout the service. I was glad that I wasn't scheduled to minister in the counseling room.

After service I quickly made my way to the car. In approximately fifteen minutes I was driving into the parking lot of my destination. I sat in the car until most of the people had come out. I made my way to a gentleman who was getting in his car alone and asked him if Mother Craig was still inside. He responded, "Yes, I believe she is." I could not believe it. This woman was supposedly incarcerated. I decided to sit a few more minutes, hoping to get a glimpse of this woman that I didn't even know, but had formed an image and an opinion of. As I sat there my emotions were doing somersaults. I felt angry, betrayed, nervous, and now I was running out of patience. Rather than sit there any longer, I decided to drive by the house since I had the address with me. I arrived and spotted the address on the curb, so I parked across from the house, a few feet down and waited. I wanted desperately to put a face with the woman that I had heard such awful things about. The house looked desolate and unoccupied. Immediately I sensed a spirit of oppression. The grounds were barren and dusty and it was hard to tell whether the windows were covered with paper or some type of thin fabric. For a moment my heart felt heavy. Mother Craig never showed up and I had no desire to wait in that environment another second. In retrospect, it was probably a bogus address.

On Monday night I dialed Mother Craig's number. I don't know why, but when she answered, I was shocked. It was the voice of the same lady that I had spoken to when I first met Viv. I quickly apologized for dialing the wrong number and hung up. I was incensed and that is putting it mildly. With everything else on my plate, I surely didn't need to have to deal with trying to figure this one out. I wondered what this was coming to. I had caught this woman in a lie, but why was she lying about her mother's whereabouts? A million possibilities raced through my mind. Either this woman had squirmed her way out of jail again, or she was never in jail from the start. When Viv called that evening, I let the voicemail pick up. This would start her to thinking. I did not want to talk right now. I needed some concrete answers, but I also needed time to sort this thing out so I wouldn't lose my cool altogether. I called Mother Craig's house again on Tuesday morning. The same voice answered. I wanted to talk to this lady, but what would I say? Again I mumbled, "Sorry…wrong number." I knew that I did not want to, nor could I afford to get caught up in this absolute madness!

In the meantime, Viv called relentlessly, but I never picked up the phone. Finally on Wednesday morning after clogging my voicemail with messages, she showed up at the house full of apologies and ready to talk. She pleaded for forgiveness. Would I please forgive her for withholding Warren's full name? When I informed her that I had called her mother's home, she acted as if she did not have a clue what I was talking about. I proceeded to let her know that her mom's number registered on my caller ID the last three times that she called me that morning. Her answer was that she was only there fifteen minutes. I told her that the time frame was over a period of two hours. Suddenly selective amnesia set in and she couldn't remember how long she was there. My insides began to boil. I did not want to continue talking to her, but I knew it was needful. When we sat down to talk, it was like wading through quicksand. The apologies were unending and I was unmoved. She started trying to manipulate the situation with sighing and tears until I got righteously indignant and told her what I had discovered. She then came out with the story that she had thrown a fit about the judge being so hard on her mom and convinced him to honor her request to grant her mother a weekend pass. She was haunted with how bad her mom looked and how she was going downhill. So, she went to church with her mom to meet with Bishop Tyler and his wife. Apparently this was as a result of the letter that she wrote to the Bishop. Her mom repented and asked forgiveness, but spent their time alone tearing her dad apart and disclosing ugly things about him. She claimed that Babbi withdrew and was petrified. When she tried to make the child talk to her mom, she saw the terror on her face and realized it was not a good idea.

---

*Holy Spirit is always trying to get our attention, trying to divert our way **before** we hit the brick wall head on. Oftentimes, instead of following His leading, we get out ahead of Him and in essence try to get Him to validate and follow carnality. When Jesus departed to go back to the Father, He said, "I'm going to send you another Helper"* ***(John 16:7 (NKJV)***. *He left Holy Spirit here for our benefit. He is that Helper and Counselor. He guides us into all truth and shows us things to come **(vs.13)**, if we will allow Him. He is all of the help that we need, but He will not violate our wills. If God will warn the heathen, how much more will He give warning to His children?*

---

2 Chronicles 36:15-16 (NKJV)

I look back at the multiple times when I got a "check" in my spirit that certain things were not right, but being busy with my own life, I failed to yield. It wasn't that I lacked discernment. My "vacuum cleaner of life" was constantly running and drowning out the Voice of Reason, and because of my need to be savior to someone who was out to sever my jugular, I could not hear. Or maybe I did not want to hear. Sometimes we are so afraid of being wrong. No one wants to miss it! Facing the fact that we've been naïve or that someone could actually "get over" on us gives the appearance that we don't have it all together. What a misnomer! Jesus the Christ is the only perfect One. For the rest of us… get used to missing the mark!

Members of my family could not understand how I could have been taken by this woman's scheme. No matter how sharp others think you are or how sharp you believe you are **"Even the Elect can be Deceived."** We have an enemy and one of his names is **"Deceiver."** He can and will use anybody that will avail themselves. People are used everyday to get the work of the enemy done in this earth realm. Sadly enough, many Christians lend themselves to Satan's plots and ploys, and don't even realize it. This person called herself a **Christian**, yet she wallowed in deception and obviously enjoyed deceiving everyone that she came in contact with. A Christian? One has to question the ingenuity of that claim. This person has her own definition of Christianity; the counterfeit version. Jesus said, "These people draw near to me with their mouth, and honor me with their lips, but their heart is far from me."...**Matthew 15:8**. I am reminded of several scriptures that warn us of Satan's devices and his ability to make the counterfeit look so legitimate...so real. The apostle Paul speaks of this:

"For such are false apostles [spurious, counterfeits], deceitful workmen, masquerading as apostles (special messengers) of Christ (the Messiah). And it is no wonder, for Satan himself masquerades as an angel of light".

2 Corinthians 11:13-14 (Amplified)

The coming [of the lawless one, the antichrist] is through the activity and working of Satan and will be attended by great power and with all sorts of [pretended] miracles and signs and delusive marvels – [all of them] lying wonders.

2 Thessalonians 2:9 (Amplified)

In the book of **Revelation 13:2-4**, the Apostle John gives us another account of Satan's wickedness and ability to be the great impostor; "A beast coming up out of the sea with ten horns and seven heads."

"Now the beast which I saw was like a leopard, his feet were like the feet of a bear, and his mouth like the mouth of a lion. The dragon gave him his power, his throne, and great authority. And I saw one of his heads as if it had been mortally wounded, and his deadly

wound was healed. And all the world marveled and followed the beast.

So they worshipped the dragon who gave authority to the beast; and they worshipped the beast, saying, "Who is like the beast? Who is able to make war with him?"

Then I saw another beast coming up out of the earth, and he had two horns like a lamb and spoke like a dragon. And he exercises all the authority of the first beast in his presence, and causes the earth and those who dwell in it to worship the first beast, who's deadly wound was healed.

He performs great signs, so that he even makes fire come down from heaven on the earth in the sight of men.

And he deceives those who dwell on the earth by those signs- (vss. 11-14) NKJV

In all three accounts we see Satan (who is also called the *dragon*) being the source of assistance to deceive the souls of many. The second beast, which came forth from the earth, looked like a lamb, but when he opened his mouth, he sounded like a dragon. Those are two completely opposite natures encompassing the same person; the devourer in sheep's clothing.

I am reminded of the account in **(Exodus 7: 9-12) NKJV.**

God, knowing that the Pharoah would demand a sign from Moses and Aaron when he was confronted by them to let God's people go, instructed Aaron through Moses to cast down his rod. Aaron's rod became a serpent. The Pharoah, who would not be outdone, called his wizards, sorcerers, and magicians to do likewise. Their rods also became serpents, but Aaron's rod swallowed them up. Twice more the Pharoah's magicians were able to perform counterfeit miracles. The first plague that was called upon the Egyptians was, the water turned to blood. The magicians were also able to turn water to blood. The second was the plague of frogs. The magicians also replicated this plague, but went overboard, making what was horrific even worse. Then God drew a line in the sand. Beyond that the magicians powers ceased to produce, and they were unable to replicate any of the other plagues. Throwing their hands up, they had to acknowledge that their limited power was no match for the **limitless** power of the Almighty God! They had received their power through Satan, who is able to emulate the miraculous, and even tell the future with a degree of accuracy through familiar spirits.

The deceptive influence of the enemy is world wide, and as believers we are not exempt. **(Revelation. 12:9)** In order for prophecy to be fulfilled there will be deception, regardless to whether or not we believe it or accept it. That is the word of God. We are the sanctified; the set apart for God's holy service. We are the **elect**. The Greek word is **eklektos**; Those who have received the gift of God, and have obtained salvation through our Lord, Jesus Christ, and through repentance have given up the life of sin and turned to Him. Why wouldn't we be the enemy's prime target? He already has the world on his team. They are no threat to his kingdom, but we are.

In his craftiness and subtleties Satan has such a broad range of tactics, which we will expound on later.

I am in awe as I go back through my journal and read the day by day accounts of the continual drama. I realize that many of the stories that Viv rigged up were to evoke a reaction from me. I believe it ignited her adrenaline and the rush must have done to her what drugs do to junkies. I did not know it then, but the woman was a pathological liar, who cleverly wore the appearance of a poor little victimized helpless creature needing to be rescued or she would not survive.

After one of my long Fridays working at our Community Outreach Program, Viv surprised me. My guess is that she had come to her end of "what to do next." I had just picked Babbi up from school when she called to find out when I would be home. I told her I was on my way. When I arrived she met me in the parking area with a big smile on her face. I walked ahead of her through the back door of my utility room and there was a brand new top of the line Whirlpool washer and dryer. Attached was a letter expressing her love and gratitude and acknowledging her shortcomings. I didn't know what to say, except "Thank you very much." I was certainly in need of those appliances, and deserving of them, I might add. We visited the Laundromat each week to wash, so I was a happy camper.

The holidays were drawing near and Deirdre and I were looking forward to going home to be with our family for Christmas. Since mom and dad had moved back to their birth place in North Carolina, we were now doing the circular trip. I have such fond memories of those days. We would start in early October scouting for reasonable fares, and we always hit the jackpot! We would stay with my son Derek and his family, visit my brothers and their families, spend some time with friends, and then the day after Christmas we would head out to see mom and dad.

One night I mentioned to Viv that it was near time to get our airline tickets for home. Believing that her money was all tied up I knew she could not afford the trip for both she and Babbi. I felt bad for the child when Viv began telling me how her mother was like Scrooge and that they were not allowed to put up decorations to celebrate Christmas in her home. She said that Babbi had not enjoyed a real Christmas since they moved to LA. Of course hearing this grieved my heart. To deprive a child of one of the utmost joys…I could not conceive of that. I decided that in spite of everything, I would see to it that this would be a Christmas they would not forget. Our family gatherings were always so wonderful and so special. I was the eldest of seven children -five boys and two girls. one brother died in infancy and another brother was shot to death by a mentally ill person. My only sister lived next door to my parents, and my three brothers and their families still live in Philly. As the eldest child, I cannot remember one Christmas that wasn't filled with great joy and exuberance. Mom loved to cook all kinds of foods and bake all kinds of goodies. I would brag to friends about her five specialty cakes that she would line up across her buffet. She poured her all into making holidays (especially Christmas) a very festive and memorable time for our family. I would watch her take such care and time preparing so that every family moment together was special and memorable. It really did not matter whether it was the holidays or Sunday dinner, her love oozed out of every morsel. On Christmas day the house was filled with my siblings and their spouses, all of the children, grandchildren, and beaucoup relatives. The house was like Grand Central Station, not to mention the countless friends that dropped by to get a slice or two of their favorite cakes. There was always room for one more at my parent's home. As far back as I can remember, there was always a relative or an orphaned friend living with us. My parents came to the rescue of my youngest brother's best friend who was fifteen at the time. His foster mother was having major surgery and could no longer keep him. Mom and dad did not want to see him go back into the system and they did not want to be foster parents, so they started the paperwork and adopted him. I knew that Viv and Babbi would be more than welcome to join our family for Christmas.

I had been sharing with my mother some of the bazaar things that were happening to this poor victimized woman. Mom trusted my decision to embrace Viv and her child. I had always been the responsible one who displayed sound judgment. I didn't consider myself all that "streetwise", but I pretty much had been able to spot a con. This time was different. I was on assignment for the kingdom of God, and Satan knew it. He was out to stop me at any cost, and I was none the wiser.

I am convinced that the enemy studies us so that he knows just how to come and what specific bait to use. Just in the natural, when there is war, the adversary would be at a total disadvantage if he did not study his opponent; how much more in this spiritual warfare that we walk out daily as children of God? Had Viv come alone she would never have gotten as far with me as she did, but with a child added to the equation ....Voila! Mission accomplished!! Babbi was a child with many needs and Deirdre and I seized the opportunity to sow into her little life. No matter who you are, you are already deceived if you think that you are exempt from deception, and especially if you have a God given assignment that you are out to fulfill.

We still had a production to mount; a huge mailing to get out for the upcoming season, and our culminating showcases for each class were in rehearsals. Besides that, both Deirdre and I were working late nights. I called and talked to my son Derek and his wife Penny about some of the things that were going on. We would be staying with them and my four grandsons when we got to Philly. My daughter in-law assured me that any decision I made was fine with her and my son was in agreement. I wanted Viv and Babbi to have a wonderful holiday season. I didn't want to leave them behind. Even with all of the drama and the frustration that came with it, I wanted to make this holiday season most memorable for them. After all I had embraced them as my new found family, and up until now I was convinced that God had placed them in my life and me in theirs. **Can the Elect be Deceived?** You bet!

In one of many letters overflowing with terms of endearment, Viv wrote a poem on the cover page addressing me as the "Anointed woman and gift from God". She went on to quote an arsenal of scriptures and proclaim that "without Jesus it is dark and empty; everything is temporary and there is no inner peace." Overall the poem sounded so eloquent and sincere, but the bottom line is that Satan can and does quote scripture. When Jesus told him in **Matthew. 4:4 *(NKJV)***, "It is written" and quoted the Word, Satan came right back at Jesus in ***vs. 6*** saying, "It is written" and he also quoted the Word. Viv was like the fig tree that Jesus cursed. She was living a continual lie!

.

At this point I can't remember when Viv was released from "protective custody", but she was back home by Thanksgiving and for more reasons than one, I was a wee bit relieved. It had been many years since I had been responsible for a now six-year-old, and those two months seemed like two years.

In the weeks that followed more names were added to the cast of "deception.". Judge Lee lived in a small town in South Carolina. Viv claimed that her dad worked for him for years and that they had a very special relationship. He was so moved by her dad's death that he would do anything to make things easier for her. She said that he was retired and would oversee the trailer park property and see that her rent was collected each month until she found someone that she could trust to do it. Rus Dolbert from McColl, S.C. would take care of any maintenance and keep the grounds. Ella Mae Grace now appears as Viv's **real** mother. This was revealed during court. Mother Craig announced that she was not her birth mother, but Ella Mae Grace was. Viv knew her as a very close friend of the family. The court was informed that Viv was given to Mother Craig by Ella when she was three months old.

We worked diligently to get everything finished and in order before our trip. Surprisingly Viv was a great help, as she actually stepped up to the plate and took over the bulk mailing after I showed her how to prepare it. When I got home from work one night she had done all of the labeling, sorting, and banding. Ninety percent of the work was done, and I could concentrate on other areas of need. It worked out that Viv and Babbi were going to make the trip with us after all. By the time the decision was made the fares had increased. My mom helped us out and dad was also in agreement. I still have the letter that mom had to fax to the travel agency authorizing the use of her credit card. It was understood that this would be a loan. From some of the things that I shared, mom thought that change would be a good thing for them. More than that, I think that my folks heard my heart concerning this situation and they were sensitive to it.

I left for my trip ahead of everyone else. Deirdre had a few more days at work and Viv had to wait until Babbi was out of school, so they would all be traveling together.

I looked forward to the four days that I would have with my grandsons to unwind and enjoy them before Viv and Babbi arrived. They arrived with Deirdre on December 21st, and Derek and I picked them up. They had no trouble fitting in. Derek and Penny made them feel right at home. Babbi and the boys hit it off and had a great time together. Viv adored children and she fell in love with the baby. Reminding her again and again not to hold him so much, was like talking to a teen-ager. She was spoiling him and I knew that his mom and dad would have a hard time after we left. The drama stayed undercover while we were in Philly. It was being stored up for North Carolina.

The four of us left the day after Christmas, heading to North Carolina to visit my parents. The flight was just a little over an hour and dad picked us up at the airport. When we arrived at home, mom had everything laid out and waiting for us. She welcomed our new family with opened arms and lots of love. We learned that my niece, Angel and her long time sweetheart had decided to get married there on New Year's Day. After a super delicious dinner, we exchanged gifts and I encouraged Viv to share parts of her story with my folks.

Viv had a cell phone and the second day of our visit with my parents, she informed me that Judge Evans had called and would be coming into South Carolina. The story continues and the circus comes to town. Part of the cast arrested in LA was brought to South Carolina. to be tried. What!? They were her sisters Corina, Danine, Nynah, and Lucille, her brother Jerry, and Mother Craig. Why they were being brought back to South Carolina to be tried was beyond me, but I didn't ask any questions. Sometimes I just did not want to hear her answers, and this was one of those times. She claimed to have spoken to Judge Lee, and was to meet him, retrieve her belongings and get her business straight. Some of the business that he was referring to was a $100,000. Life Insurance policy supposedly left to Viv by Warren. She named the insurance company and said that she was told by a representative that she would only need his death certificate and her ID to finalize everything. Her belongings also included the past eight months rent from all tenants in the trailer park, a three carat diamond ring that she bought for her mother the year before, and an undetermined amount of cash. My feeling about this whole thing was that these lawmakers were taking their authority a bit far, but again I held my peace. I was on vacation. Why did they need to follow her across the country? Why couldn't this wait a few weeks? They were like a pack of ravenous wolves. This had to be all about money. We were in North Carolina until January 4th, but a lot would take place in that time.

One morning after breakfast Viv informed me that Judge Lee called and wanted to know if she could meet him at a certain location to pick up her things. I asked my dad, and of course he was glad to help her out. As I remember, she came up with Carolina Beach, as a meeting place. The name of the restaurant escapes me now, but the judge would meet us in the parking lot at 2:00 p.m. She knew exactly how to get there. It was a seafood restaurant surrounded by water with a large parking area fenced in on two sides by large logs. We sat in the car talking and waiting for the car that she had described to arrive. After fifteen minutes or so, we got out to stretch our legs. It was a beautiful December day. We watched the seagulls take off and land around the parking lot. I was so hopeful that this woman would finally get her things. When I wondered out loud what was keeping the judge, she made a call and told us that Judge Lee was running late, but was on his way. One hour later the judge was still on his way. Though dad was so patient and didn't seem to mind, I was getting anxious. I didn't want to believe that someone else that she trusted would disappoint her again. Most of all, I did not want my dad's time wasted.

The judge never showed, and we ended up in South Carolina! It took us two and a half hours to get there, and again, she directed dad all the way. Our first stop was Beckford's Funeral home. She asked to stop there and pick up Warren's death certificate. When we got there, she first went across the street to the Beckford's home. I remember thinking, "Oh, she knows these people personally." After a few minutes she came out with a middle–aged woman whom she followed up some stairs into the funeral parlor. Five minutes later she came out sulking and looking as if she would explode. As she climbed into the back seat of the car, I asked what happened. She burst into tears and in between gulping breaths, she said, "Evans and Lee have been here and picked up the death certificate." I asked, "What now?" She said that Mrs. Beckford told her to go to the Department of Records to get another copy. I could tell that dad was upset. He hated seeing her cry and he did not like the idea that those men were using their power to take advantage of her. Viv directed us to the Department of Records a short distance away. When we arrived she went inside, but after a few minutes, came back to the car empty-handed. Her countenance was so disturbing that I cannot remember the reason that she gave for failing to get the death certificate. She attempted several times to contact Judge Lee, but told us there was no answer. She gave directions to his home in a beautiful area overlooking a big lake. Dad parked where she told him and she walked across the street and went to one of the homes. Again she came back in tears and told us that his wife said he was called out of town suddenly and would be in Columbia until the next day. She was angry and asked if we would to take her to the sheriff's department to file a complaint. By now dad and I were both worked up about this situation, and the sheriff's department seemed like the only solution to this continual charade. She asked someone for directions and within twenty minutes we were there. We sat in the car and waited for her. It was not long before she came back with her countenance unchanged, and told us that they were giving her the run around, making excuses for the judge, and trying to convince her to take an alternate route. She told us that everyone in town knew Judge Lee, and they don't want to make waves. Now to me, that sounded about right for a small town in the south. The last stop that we made was at the church that she once attended. I can't even remember why we went there, but I am sure it was all connected. The sanctuary was closed, but I recall a bible study was letting out from a long trailer across the grounds on the other side. Viv went over and greeted some of the people, then bought them over to the car to meet dad and myself. It was dark now and I felt like we wasted a lot of time, and accomplished nothing but a "wild goose chase." I didn't make the connection then, but her mission had been accomplished. She had gotten her South Carolina visits in. I believe she knew someone at each stop that we made, and she worked a story line so that she could get those visits in. The tears, the anger, the frustration, the anxiety was all an Academy award winning con.

After five hours round-trip and probably eight or nine hours total, we arrived back at home. Mom had dinner waiting and as we shared the events of the day, I cannot describe the look on my mother's face. Maybe she didn't like hearing that we had such a barren day, or was it that she felt our disgust and frustration for the spectacle that Viv had become? It was none of the above. Mom had picked up on something, but she kept silent about it. She told me much later that she knew something was not right, but never thought the outcome would be so unbelievable. None of us did.

For the next couple of days we were busy with preparations for my niece, Angel's wedding. I was haunted with the fact that we would go back to LA empty handed and without accomplishing anything. Viv claimed that she got a call from Judge Evans saying that he was in South Carolina and had picked up her things from Judge Lee. He had also gotten in touch with her real mom, Ella, who would like to see her. Viv wanted her things, but the idea of coming face to face with her mom seemed to make her anxious. My mother assured her that it would be okay if she wanted to invite her to come to the house. Viv kept saying that she did not want to see her, but she wanted her things. Supposedly there were calls back and forth. I even heard her repeating the directions that dad had given her to the house, but no one ever showed up. It turned out to be a repeated fiasco.

Viv talked to me that night about how blessed she was to have my family and me…people who loved and cared about her. She was so sorry for the way things turned out, for us having gotten the runaround, and in her words, "for believing those snakes and their lies." She appeared genuinely remorseful. She expressed her concern to me about other property that belonged to her dad. She told me that he loved antiques and that his house was filled with his collectibles. She said that she did not care for antiques, but she wanted me to have them. She was sure that her dad's estate would be straightened out soon and asked if I would come back with her in a few months to help her organize. I told her that I could not make that commitment. I was hopeful that she would go back alone and get her business straight. She named items that she wanted my dad to have. They included a John Deere tractor with all attachments, mule trailer, riding lawn mower, and power and manual tools. She told me that a good friend of her dad's named Simon who was the new fire chief in that town would be given the keys to the property and the garage. She would Fed-ex copies of the keys to him when she got back to Los Angeles. She talked to my dad and asked him if he would accept her gifts and auction off anything that he did not want. She told dad about Simon and asked if she could give Simon the phone number so they could discuss matters. I kept the letter that she wrote and had notarized stating that my dad should be mediator for an auction of the things that he chose not to keep. I had shared with her that my dad did some farming and was about to purchase a tractor. This was "right on time" information for her and she used it to disguise compensating dad for the drama that she caused, when in essence, it was just another measure of deceit.

After returning to LA, things became more of a circus than ever and the cast continued to grow. Viv's belongings changed hands more times than I can recall. Judge Lindsey was introduced as another long-time family friend who had teamed up with Lee. Viv was told that there was no need to worry now, because Lindsey would take care of everything and have her things sent right away. Even though Judge Evans was still in South Carolina, he was supposedly easing Viv's misfortune by arranging for her to receive the rents from Mother Craig's roomers. Viv claimed that her name was on the title deed and that she planned to eventually sell the house. She claimed that Judge Evans was under fire by the other judges (Lindsey and Lee) for making things difficult for her.

On the Saturday after returning home, we spent the day unpacking and washing clothes..

Viv announced that she had called Mother Craig's tenants to let them know that she would be by to pick up their rents. She said one of the tenants (Sandy) asked her to come later, when her husband would be in from work. I loaned Viv my car and reminded her that we had to leave early in the morning for church. She would be returning to her new member's classes and had only two left to complete. As the story evolved, when Viv arrived there were no rents to be picked up. A phone call came from Judge Evans and she was informed that her money had been directly deposited to a well-known bank a couple of miles from the house. She could go there on Monday morning and it would be released to her. After taking Babbi to school on Monday, Viv claimed to have gone to that bank and found that the judge had opened an account in her name, but had also put his name on it. Both signatures were needed to withdraw the money. What a joke.

Before the end of the month the cast included Superior Judge Smith, (who was handling things in Evans' stead) and Judge Kidd. Attorney Powell came on board, highly recommended by Viv's former pastor (Hedges) in South Carolina. Attorney Powell received Viv's things from Judge Lindsey and would represent Viv. Her "real mother", Ella arrived in LA and found her way to Mother Craig's house to inquire of Viv's whereabouts. Connie, who lived next door, actually took Ella to the courthouse after she announced that she was Viv's real mother. Superior Judge Smith called Connie in and warned her not to get involved. According to Viv, Ella caused a ruckus at the courthouse, and Viv obtained a restraining order. Ella raised the roof about it, got herself in trouble and ended up being arrested.

In the meantime, court is being held concurrently in South Carolina.

The meeting with Simon and my dad never happened. Viv claimed that she spoke with him several times, but she always seemed to have a story as to why he had not made contact with dad. It didn't seem to matter to my dad and he never inquired as to what happened. I asked him once about it and he said that he never heard from the guy.

We never mentioned it again. However, Simon does make another appearance later in this script.

One Saturday morning as I was leaving for the studio Viv informed me that she had just called Attorney Powell because she had not heard from him. She said that he had lied to Judges Smith and Lindsey about being in touch with her. His live-in maid answered and when Viv identified herself, she was asked to hold on. When the maid came back to the phone, she announced that Powell was out of town and was not expected back until Monday. Viv felt that the lady was lying. After a few hours she called back and said that Powell answered the phone and was nearly speechless. She confronted him and told him that she could not trust him because he was a liar and a deceiver. Imagine that. As mother would say, "Listen to the frying pan calling the kettle black." As the story unfolds, Powell began to sound like Evans. He told Viv that the reason he had not sent her things was because she asked that they be sent in my name, and he had a problem with that. He told her that my daughter and I were going to take her down and strip her of everything. She blew up and told him that she was sick and tired of everyone accusing me when they were the culprits. This did not move me in the least. My heart was right, my motives were pure, and my hands were clean. I only wanted to do everything in my power to secure and recover what we had loaned Viv. We had worked hard and I owed that to my daughter. Neither of us was looking for anything beyond or above what we had put out. Viv called Powell a "snake" after he admitted that they had investigated to find out if there were any drugs involved with her dad's estate. The insinuation that her dad could not possibly have obtained his wealth legally really set her off. When she told him that she would talk to Lindsey, he promised that he would do whatever she wants and there would be no need to speak with the judge. Viv said she went to see Superior Judge Smith and filled him in on the situation with Powell, then asked him to call Lindsey. Both judges were upset by Powell's behavior and scheduled a conference call. They listened while Powel hung himself. He told them that he had touched bases with Viv daily, that she was doing fine, and that he had mailed her things right after he got them. Powell was confronted, deemed incompetent and threatened with expulsion. Powell had also lied about there being an investigation.

As I struggled to come up with a solution to this madness, I envisioned a pocket with multiple holes in it. It seemed that every time this woman got close to retrieving her things, they fell through another hole. It was as though she had become a plaything at our expense. To say that I was frustrated is an understatement. I presented to Viv what I thought might be somewhat of a solution, at least a partial one. I asked if there was a responsible tenant that she knew at the trailer park who was trustworthy. Someone who would collect all rents, issue receipts and send them to her via registered mail. I suggested that compensation could be in the form of a rent reduction or whatever she felt comfortable with. She thought about it and came up with a lady named Grace. I asked her a few questions regarding this person, such as how long she had known her, how long she had been a tenant, and if she paid on time, etc.

She was positive that Grace was the one. She told me that she would call and offer her the job. Her story was that after speaking with Grace and offering a rent reduction of fifty percent, Grace accepted the position and it was all set. Viv asked if I would compose a letter detailing their agreement because she did not know how to word it. I composed a simple letter thanking Grace for accepting the job, reiterating the compensation agreement, stating the acceptable forms of payment and that they be made payable to Viv. The package was to be sent to Viv via registered mail only. As I wrote the letter she prepared a tenant list totaling thirty-three units. The names looked authentic and only two surnames were repeated on the list. The last names ranged from names like, Adams to Wilson.

I prepared a second letter to the tenants informing them of the recent changes, reiterating the acceptable forms of payment made payable to Viv, and asking that payments be submitted to Grace who was acting representative for the property owner. The next day, we went to the studio and made copies of the letter to Grace and copies for her to distribute to the tenants. The letters were mailed early giving plenty of time for the adjustment. Or should I say that, I assumed the letters were mailed.

Newsflash - according to Viv, Attorney Powell is suddenly missing and so are her belongings that he supposedly mailed. When he was a no-show for court, a visit was made to his home. His wife appeared shocked and said that she had not seen him since he left for court that morning. Now the authorities were searching everywhere, including the airlines. Police were on the lookout in Sumpter and Kershaw.

What could possibly be next?

By mid-week I had to leave for Vegas again. Getting away was good for me, and ministering to my friend Jo was a blessing that I thoroughly enjoyed. Viv took me to the airport and kept my car. That evening within a few hours of my arrival in Vegas, she called to report the latest. Mother Craig, who was among those incarcerated in South Carolina, had called my home twice. After calling and reporting this to Judge Smith, Viv went to see him and together they called Lindsey who was not aware of Mother Craig's release. Viv activated the voicemail and both judges listened to the two messages that were left. Smith had Lindsey check out whether Mother Craig was still incarcerated, and the answer was "No!" She had been released two weeks prior. Ella was also released from jail, and promised to go back to Sumpter and never return to LA. In the meantime, it's way past the time that we should have received the rents from the trailer park. I expected a new beginning because the rents from Mother Craig's roomers were also supposedly in the mail. This time Viv claimed that she spoke to each tenant and they all told her that their rents were mailed on the third of the month.

I was still in Vegas when Viv called to say that the rents from South Carolina had not arrived yet. There had to be a good reason why they had not arrived, I thought...Perhaps Grace had not followed instructions to send the envelope via registered mail. Would she have sent the rent from thirty-three people via regular mail? Viv asked if I thought that she should call Judge Lee and ask him to get involved since Grace did not seem to be reliable. This was just ludicrous... the epitome of insanity! I could not believe the unending chain of events, and more than that, I could not believe that I was in the midst of them. As I listened with a calloused ear, I envisioned the future; trying to imagine what a year from this moment would bring. The situation was out of control! I had to make a quick decision not to engage or unleash my emotions to match it.

My advice to Viv was to leave Lee out of it. I told her it was best that he did not know anything since she had assumed the responsibility to take care of it. Viv could not get in touch with Grace, so she thought of her friend Pam in Sumpter, SC who called her at the house sometimes. She called Pam and asked her to go by and give Grace a message, but she declined. She did not want to get involved because she felt that it would cause strife. The only thing left to do was call Grace again and find out if the mail was sent properly, which Viv claimed to have done. Now with bills due, and over due, we faced the frustration and uncertainty of another waiting period.

I did a lot of praying that weekend, both for the situation at hand and for my friend Jo who was having such a hard time. It was my last day there and one of the most difficult visits to Vegas that I ever had. A lot was going on with her health and she was very tearful. The stroke caused her to have emotional outbursts that just broke my heart. It was my first time having to take her sugar level, which meant poking her several times a day. After the morning routine and exercise, it was heavy on my heart to pray with her. On my knees in front of her wheelchair, I took her hands in mine, and told her that we must pray. She was able to talk, although her speech was slurred at times. I reminded her how much she was loved and asked if she would pray with me. She shook her head to say, "Yes." I asked her to repeat after me, and she moved her lips, but nothing came out. I encouraged her to let God hear her words, but she burst into a blood-curdling sob and I knew the enemy was attacking. I continued to pray hoping she would follow, but she dropped her head and closed her eyes. Silently my own tears fell. Pastor J. came home not long after and

I headed for the airport. Jo began to cry again as I said, "goodbye", which always made it even harder for me to leave.

Viv picked me up at the airport and filled me in on the continuing drama.

According to her, Pam had changed her mind and agreed to help her out. Grace still had the package containing the rents, and agreed to give it to Pam so that she could mail it. However, at the tail end of the report, Pam had gone by three times to pick up the package, but Grace did not answer the door or the phone. None of the calls that Viv claimed to have made were ever made in my presence. I let her know that I was aware of this, but of course there was always a cock-a-mamie story behind why that was.

In the next few days, I was told that Judge Smith informed all of the roomers at Mother Craig's that they would need to pay or move. With no sign of Powell, and his whereabouts remaining unknown, we definitely had a suspense drama in the works here. I wondered every day how this would finally play out. The actor in me kept saying…."This would make a crazy drama."

The craftiness of Satan working through this woman was amazing. She was so excited about going to church the next morning, and I was excited for her. She had started this journey in August, and now it was February. She would finally be fellow-shipped in as a new member. The service was great, and we were really proud of Viv as she walked to the microphone, spoke her name and received the right hand of fellowship. Her decision to start over and get this done was a milestone in itself. She had missed some classes while in "protective custody" and had to wait for them to recycle. At one time I was doubtful that it would ever happen. We wanted to take her to brunch after church, but our first board meeting of the year took precedence. At the studio, Viv helped us set up and I loaned her my car to go to the mall. After the meeting she returned with a Valentine's Day gift for me and the report that Powell was found in Florida. The authorities who found him were accompanied by Lindsey. However, the news of his arrest came from none other than Simon. Remember him...her dad's Fire Chief friend? He gave Viv the scoop. He also told her that Lindsey confided in him that he was troubled by a comment that she had made a few days before, that if she had been white, she would have her belongings and more by now.

I marvel at how the spirit of deception was so meticulously positioned, giving credence to the situations and circumstances with such detail and precision.

A few examples: For Viv to appear so sincere about wanting the gift of Holy Spirit; to beg me to act as durable power of attorney and to actually pay the attorney's fee to have it drawn up; to fabricate the time of a parent's death and the circumstances surrounding it; to call from an airport making things appear authentic; to set an appointment and to have a Realtor come to my home and go over the terms and particulars of selling property that belonged to someone else; and finally to take all of the necessary steps to join and become a member of my church with such determination...Satan personified.

14.
Maximized Mockery

Viv was to meet with the Realtor the next day to discuss the sale of Mother Craig's property, but she began to have chest pains and canceled.

Her story was that the buyer (who offered $8,000.00 above the listing price) also wanted to meet her at the house to go over a few things. I told her that was the job of the agent. I had actually met the agent when Viv had him come to the house the first time. He was from a large and very reputable agency.

She introduced us and he gave me one of his cards. She asked me if I had a moment to listen to what he had to say. As I remember, he had a profile of the house with him. He asked her a few questions, went over some figures, and gave her some information. After that I excused myself to catch up on some paperwork. In retrospect, I have no reason to doubt that the agent was not legit, though I did get the feeling that he was being patronizing and tolerant with her. It seemed that the guy thought she may be wasting his time and he wanted to hurry and be done with the appointment.

Viv began to have chest pains again and I laid hands on her and prayed. I was prepared to take her to the hospital if it continued, but she decided to take her nitroglycerin and lie down. Following her instructions, I gave her three tabs, five minutes apart. As she lay there, she mentioned being upset with Grace for not releasing the package to Pam. Feeling better, a few hours later she knocked on my bedroom door to say that she had called Simon and asked him to pick up her package from Grace and give it to Pam. He went to Grace's house, but got no answer. By now, I'm not surprised or moved by what is happening. I had chose to remain optimistic in spite of it all. I had not yet faced the fact that this woman could be capable of such beguiling acts.

One positive thing happened when the mail situation was straightened out. Viv started getting her child support and disability checks at my P.O. Box. I took her to pick up the checks, and then to the bank where she purchased a money order for $309.00 to make a payment on the washer and dryer that she gave me. I wondered why such a steep payment on the appliances, but my guess was that she wanted to pay it off as soon as possible. I didn't ask any questions, nor was I about to discourage that. After a discussion about the situation with the rents in Sumpter, we decided to get letters in the mail to all tenants right away. Everyone would be informed that Grace was released from all responsibility and be asked to send their payment for the next month's rent to the post office box. Again, I prepared the letters; one to Grace and the other to all thirty-three tenants. I must admit that I have serious doubts that any of the mail addressed to Sumpter ever got there. The truth is, I never witnessed Viv actually mailing anything.

Being three days now since Powell's capture, Viv is upset with Judge Smith because he has yet to call and give her the news. Simon told her that Smith was the first person that Lindsey called with the report. Viv started complaining of feeling ill again. She called her doctor and got an appointment for that evening. After we picked Babbi up from school, I drove her to the doctor's and she was hospitalized. Her doctor was a resident at one of LA's most renowned hospitals and his office was just a few blocks away. I stayed with her while they administered an I.V. and did an Ekg, which caused some concern. Nearly five hours later, I took Babbi home and gave her dinner and a bath before putting her to bed. At 12:15 am., I received a call from a woman named Ruth. She was a nurse at the hospital saying that they had been trying to reach me. I had a block on my phone, which I had forgotten about. Apparently Viv had been throwing a fit and would not let up until someone got in touch with me. Finally, the nurse called her daughter and had her to call me on a three-way and some how we were connected. By then Viv had been placed in ICU for observations, so I did not speak with her, but another nurse assured me that all was well. The chest pains had ceased, but she was battling a headache because of the nitro drops. I gave Ruth a message for Viv encouraging her to get rest.

The next morning I dropped Babbi off at school and was at the studio before 9:00 am. The first call that came in was from Viv saying that she had already talked to Lindsey. Apparently Lindsey contacted Smith and told him how Viv felt, because he called to apologize and paid her a visit at the hospital, which she believed was a move to pacify her. She also claimed to have talked to Simon, who said that Grace had been located in Winston-Salem, N.C., and was warned that she had until 5:00 pm. to get back to South Carolina with the rents from the trailer park.

After I finished at the studio, I visited Viv at the hospital and took her toiletries and clean underwear. She was still in ICU and doing well, with no chest pains and her sugar was regulated. The following day she was moved into a room. She told me that her mother (Ella) called three times and she hung up on her. Viv blamed Smith for informing Ella that she was hospitalized. He admitted that he made a mistake and did not think that Ella would harass her. His purpose was to let her know that she was somewhat the cause. After a couple of days and a series of tests, she was discharged with a ton of meds.

The next day Viv was up and about. She took Babbi to school and came back with the story that she saw Evans and his bodyguard, Bobby parked near the school. She said, "Evans ducked, but not before I saw him." The following day the story was, "I dropped Babbi off, and there was Evans, Pastor Hedges and Mr. Hedges sitting in the same car that I saw Evans in yesterday. Evans tried to convince me that we needed to talk. Pastor Hedges came towards me with open arms and I told her, don't you touch me, Judas." How ironic! This is projection in its finest form. There are people who are skilled in the ability to turn things around, place blame, and accuse others of the very behavior that they are exhibiting. Viv called others liars, snakes, and Judas; all descriptive of the very things that she herself portrayed. Sometimes I wonder what would have happened had I not suggested that Viv contact a certain renowned attorney. How long would she have reeled in the fictitious characters and when would she have run out? I recall the day that, being quite fed up with what I thought was a bunch of greedy, ruthless, egotistical, relentless people; I got the idea that this attorney could burst this thing wide open. In fact, that was my utmost objective. I made the suggestion that Viv call the law firm and give them the story. I thought for sure that this charade would be over in no time if that attorney would take her case. I also felt that this was an "attention getter" and would be of great interest to an attorney of this caliber. Viv had also threatened to take the story to the news media.

I found the number of the attorney and gave it to Viv. She claimed to have called and spoken with the secretary who told her that the head of the firm, Jacques was out of town and would not be able to assist her, but another partner, Sean was available. In her words, she met with Sean and told him all of the particulars, especially reporting the unlawful things that the lawmakers had done. Sean called the bar association immediately and an intense investigation was to be in place covering North and South Carolinas and LA. The next thing that he wanted was a detailed description in writing of the highlights of this ordeal since the beginning. The story evolves a few days later when she talked to Sean. He had been working diligently on her case, and had been in contact with Smith to inquire about some of the unethical things that were going on. Smith told him that Viv had a tendency to request certain things, and then forget what she asked them to do. When Sean called Lindsey to clarify the accusation, he was told that both Smith and Evans were liars and crooks. According to Viv, my name was being slandered by both of them. Supposedly I had been spending all of Viv's money! In her words, they claimed that she took out a second mortgage on the house, and now that I had gone through all of that money, I had her borrow $10,000.00 more. Sean asked them how that was possible, when they were guilty of tying up all of her money. He mentioned that I had been quite patient while waiting for things to manifest. On the other hand she had not acquired the property, so how could she take out a second mortgage on a house that was not hers? I got a glimmer of hope when she told me that Sean would represent me if I wanted to sue for slander. At least I would have the revenue due us for all of the trouble. Wishful thinking, but I didn't linger there. I quickly got a reality check when I thought about the time element in any legal situation. If the present situation was any indication, we would all starve to death. The whole thing was absurd. To my knowledge Viv only had her disability and the child support coming in, nothing more.

Once again the rents from both properties were held up. Sean told Viv that their office would send notices to the tenants of both properties informing them to send their rent directly to Viv, and that their letter would now override everything else. Jacques, who was out of town and too busy to get involved, suddenly gets involved. He decided that it was necessary to "walk Sean through" the whole process and would also be with them in court. Viv was bursting with excitement when she announced this bit of news. He has gotten the FBI involved, but Smith and Evans were unaware of this. They were both arrested, but were released on their own recognizance and warned about the series of charges against them. When they were told to come up with Viv's belongings, Smith initially said they were in his office, but once at his office, he remembered that he gave them to Evans, who claimed that he never had them. Jacques supposedly blew up, warning them both to stop playing games and reminding them of their fate.

Now Viv's latest report is that Jacques has enlisted the assistance of a probate attorney named Zoë. Viv was to meet with her to get familiar with what she does. I wondered why a probate attorney would be needed unless there were no documents in place to prove that her dad's property belonged solely to her.. I decided to withdraw and observe. I had my fill of it all! Jacques has read the journal requested by Sean, which chronicled the past events. He informed her that the judges planned to "take her out" and then take all that she had. He asked her if she knew what she had and she replied that she only knew what she was told. I personally did not know and did not want to know. She would throw figures around here and there, like the check for $100,000 from Warren's insurance policy supposedly left to her, and another check for the same amount that she claimed Mother Craig had tied up in a credit union. Other than that, I never asked or cared to know any details. As far as I was concerned, it was her money, and her business. All that I wanted was what belonged to us.

When it came to loaning Viv my car, I did so more often than I wanted to, and with great reservations. She needed to take care of her business and I had neither the time nor the energy to be her chauffeur. So, the day that she came home from running an errand and announced that someone had hit her from behind, I did not even flinch. I waited for her to explain, took a deep breath and went out to take a look at my Volvo. I had a little scrape that needed to be repaired in the same place where she was hit. The good news was that the person driving the rental had insurance. Praise God! To my surprise Viv had already proceeded to take care of the particulars before she broke the news to me. She came home with the paperwork that I needed for the claim, including the contact person and the emergency medical service report from the LA Fire Department proving that she had been examined for injuries. Wow….an attempt to show a level of responsibility.

It became even more frustrating as we were approaching the month of April. The chain of events stirred up a myriad of emotions; astonishment, frustration, anger, despair, violation, and resentment. I was in a place that I had never been before and I had not foreseen any of it. Funds were still being held up, but according to Viv, Jacque was putting things in place for us to leave for South Carolina on the 8th of the month so that we could get back before the start of court. According to some of the things that Viv shared, the lawmakers seemed to think that they knew more about what was best for my life than I did. I tried to be as clear as possible when relaying my time and availability to Viv; anything to avoid more drama and miscommunication. I carefully worked out a strategic plan, considering all sides and all persons with the intended purpose of taking care of business in a timely manner. Viv would inevitably come home and tell me what was discussed, and it would be totally opposite of the agreement. With a business to run, ministerial duties to perform, and preparations for our benefit production, I was filled to capacity. Hounded daily with drama drenched lies and games concerning this woman's life and business was nerve wracking, not to mention how it was interfering with my personal life.

Viv informed me that Jacque had secured our plane tickets along with a check for the car that we would lease and a check for the babysitter. I did not think that was a strange move, because I was of the impression that it was a loan against the estate. Careful not to get my hopes up, I began to disconnect. I had been quite tolerant and needed to see something manifest and that was not happening fast enough. Viv informed me that Jacque had gotten in touch with a colleague (Mr. Davis). He would meet her in South Carolina to represent her at the banks. His asking price was $10,000. I thought, truly these people have lost their minds. All of them want "a piece of the rock." Viv resented it, saying that she knew he had gotten wind of her worth. She decided that Mr. Davis could keep his services and I agreed. Of course this was another piece of her scheme to make things look authentic.

According to Viv, Jacque was still in court with another case, and she regularly expressed feelings of neglect. She wanted her belongings, which were retrieved from Judge Kidd, who had no business with them in the first place. Sean supposedly gave them to him. Now, after two weeks, Jacque is still holding her belongings without an explanation. It was frustrating not knowing his plan of action or the reason for it. She claimed to have repeatedly inquired about her things and yet he kept withholding them. When she finally got upset about it, he told her they were being held for evidence against the judges who took them. They were said to be found in Isaac's home (bodyguard to Judge Evans).

About mid-month Viv announced how happy she was that Jacque began to spend more time on her case. He claimed to be doing all that he could for her, except he was not getting any operating funds into her hands. What he seemed to accomplish was menial, and I felt that the immediate needs of his client were being neglected, therefore causing her health to suffer. I had never met Dr. Fischman, but according to Viv, we both shared the same sentiments. Viv should go in the hospital and allow them to do the necessary tests for her heart. It was not a wise decision to keep putting it off, but I understood why she kept stalling. My guess was that she would lie there stressing about all of the bills piling up and defeat the whole purpose of being hospitalized. Her blood pressure and sugar would continue to escalate and the heart palpitations would probably increase.

Judges Lee and Lindsey came to LA for court. Viv said that one of her former doctors came in with the judges to testify, but left after seeing that court was held up. Judge Smith tried unsuccessfully to see if one of the banks would release funds to give Viv some operating cash. His next suggestion was to go after emergency funds from the state. Apparently the insurance company in South Carolina withdrew their position to allow her to cash in on the policy left by Warren with all of the activity that had surfaced in this matter. Well that fits right in with the rest of the shenanigans. After applying for state funds and having a physical, she came home with cotton taped to her inner arm indicating that she had blood drawn. She said that when her sugar was checked, it was found to be extremely high, almost 500. She was warned again about the danger of walking around with her sugar level so high. She was supposed to be notified before 5:00 p.m. of the decision to distribute her funds and where to pick up the checks. In the meantime she had a brainstorm and remembered money that she claimed to have in a credit union in New York. The story was that while living there with her sister and teaching school for a couple of years, she saved this money. Once she made the phone call and gathered the information that she needed, she asked for my help with putting her request in letter form. She gave me the name of a bank officer to whom the letter was to be addressed at a Federal Credit Union in New

York City. She requested the release of monies from her savings account in the amount of $3,643.00. The contents of the letter also stated that "upon having my attorney speak with your manager today, I was informed of the necessary documents that I would need to submit. " Viv obtained copies of her South Carolina driver's license, her California ID, social security card, and credit union card. Besides this, she also had the letter notarized as requested. These are things that I actually witnessed. I must add that I never saw her mail the letter, just as I never witnessed her mailing any of the other correspondence that I assisted her with.

I realized that I had truly missed God, but admitting that was hard. It was hard for a number of reasons. First I was not in this by myself. My daughter had seen to that. She was right there with me, especially where Babbi was concerned. There were times when Viv would push a button and I would "read her mail." Dee was totally oblivious at first. She thought I was being too tough on this poor, pitiful woman. She was not fully aware of all that caused the deficiency in my patience with her. I had only shared what Viv was going through. She didn't know that I had become a near basket case dealing with this woman. Dee felt sorry for Viv and saw her as a victim; a woman who had only been mistreated, and never loved or cared for. She was all for helping her in any way that she could. Concerning finances, I would give her the scenario and the reason why Viv needed a loan. She trusted her mother's judgment, and she would always agree. Neither of us had a clue that Viv even had the potential to be a con artist. It was the most far-fetched thing. "Never judge a book by its cover." What a befitting cliché. We believed that with every passing day, things would finally come together for her and she could pay her debts and finally be on her own. Always having a heart for the deprived, we did not want to turn our backs on Viv and her child, but in reality this was not of God! The old saying, "Follow your heart" sounds poetic and even sounds somewhat romantic, but the Word of God tells us to be led by the Spirit because **"the heart is deceitful above all things, and is exceedingly perverse and corrupt, and severely, mortally sick! Who can know it [perceive,** understand, be acquainted with his own heart and mind]? (Jer.17:9 – Amplified).

This "heart" is talking about the center of our emotions, the source of passion, our wills and conscience. Since our spirit man is the only thing that gets transformed when we confess Jesus as Lord, the war is on, and is continual between that spirit man and our flesh. The heart makes us think we are doing good, when in fact we are disobedient and rebellious. It paints falsehoods. It disguises and conceals things. Not always intentionally, but nevertheless, we are often yielding to the *heart* instead of the Spirit of God. So, the heart deceives us, and too often, we are not even aware of it. We think we are okay. Can we be sure how our hearts will lead us in a moment of temptation or pressure? One can never know. Peter is a perfect example. Unlike Judas, who plotted and schemed, I don't think for one moment that Peter planned to deny Jesus. Even after Jesus assured him that he would **(Mathew. 26:34-35)**, he told Jesus in essence, "No way, I'll die first, before I will ever deny you." I believe that Peter meant that with all of his "heart." What happened? What caused Peter to change? Did he suddenly stop loving the Lord? I don't think so. Humanity kicked in and Peter had a "***change of heart***". Peter hid and watched what happened to Jesus and he made a decision that he did not want to be subjected to the same. So, when we look at the scriptures…Matthew. 26:69-75 (NKJV), we see the prophetic words of Jesus come to pass in Peter's life. He did indeed deny Jesus. Not once, not twice, but thrice! The heart can make us think we are walking in God's ways when we are *so* in error. The deception of the heart can serve as a teacher. It can teach us to never say, "***never***", because just as soon as you are so sure of "***never***", the heart will make a liar out of you. You can end up in the very place, doing the very thing that you swore against. I am a living example.

Though there is a righteous judgement, one in which we correct or admonish one another, Jesus tells us not to *judge*, that is to criticize or condemn others or we will also be *judged*… **Mathew. 7:1-2 (NKJV)**. He said that if we do this, we would receive the same in accordance to what we dealt out. It seems that the deceitful heart tricks us into believing that, "God is referring to "everyone else, but **me**." I plead guilty. I remember speaking against a sister in the Lord concerning poor choices in her personal life. I loved her, and I was hurt and angry that she was being so foolish. She had been saved seven or eight years longer than me, and I thought she should know better. Although I was several years younger in the Lord, I had heard the aforementioned scripture many times, so I was familiar with it. However, it did not prevent me from judging her. In fact, I was appalled and commenced to carry on in my own self-righteousness about her folly. I actually spoke the words to another friend that, "I would **never** do anything so stupid!" It was not too long before the prophetic words of Jesus came to pass in my life. After standing indignantly against such behavior; after judging, condemning and criticizing her, I found myself reaping according to the measure that I had dealt, and it jolted my world! I remember how I felt when Holy Spirit reminded me of the scripture. Jesus wasn't suggesting that I should not judge. He said, "Judge not!" It was a commandment! God's Word is true and He means what He says. If we judge another, we are subject to fall into the same pit. It was a hard lesson. I loved the Lord. I thought I was so good and my heart so pure because I wasn't blatantly sinning. Nevertheless, I had disobeyed the Word. The resounding truth of the matter is that with all of my "good" intentions, my heart still deceived me.

My own heart could not tell me the truth about Viv. As women we are nurturers and often become too emotionally involved to see the truth. My lying heart told me that this woman was in trouble and she needed me. The bible tells us to "keep our hearts with all diligence, for out of them flow the issues of life" **Proverbs. 4:23 (NKJV)**. We ought to guard our hearts like some of us guard our money. Life is a very precious and delicate gift. The heart, in which the issues of this gift spring from, is to be watched over, cared for and protected above all else. It is our hearts that get us into trouble with members of the opposite sex. Our hearts produce jealousies and envy causing us to covet; wanting that which belongs to another. Our hearts cause us to enter into idolatry, putting everyone and everything else before God, while yet seeking His hand instead of His face. Our hearts cause us to lie in attempt to get away with something and to manipulate in attempt to get our way about something. And it is our hearts that cause us to strike out when another disappoints or hurts us. Jesus gave us a commandment to love them, bless them, do good towards them and pray for them. Wow, Jesus...really?!" What about when we have walked around bitter and resentful, donning that beautiful "butter wouldn't melt in your mouth" mask? We deceive our own selves. The worse kind of deception is self-deception, because you are staunch in your a decision and no one can talk you out of it. The sad part about it is that you think you are right, thus no one can help you. We humans really are an enigma; very complex creatures. The fact that I cannot know my own heart is baffling to me.

In the words of Jesus,

"For out of the heart proceed evil thoughts, murders, adulteries, fornications, thefts, false witness, blasphemies."

Mat. 15:19 (NKJV)

Way back in the beginning, the bible says:

"Then the Lord saw that the wickedness of man was great in the earth, and that every intent of the thoughts of his heart was only evil continually.

Gen. 6:5 (NKJV)

For this very reason The Lord regretted having made mankind. Whether in word or in deed, sin germinates and breeds in the heart. One thing is for sure, God is the only One who can know the heart of mankind. In this, as in all things, He is infinite and unparalleled.

As the days passed we checked my post office box daily, expecting a check to come for Viv from the credit union in New York. A week passed since it was supposed to have been sent. She said that Jacque was following up on it. She claimed to have missed a day at court, because Counsel didn't bother to inform her until the last minute. Time and again the promises that the rent situation would be straightened out fell through. Time and again the stories took another dive...another detour. She brought me the news that Jacque was checking with Dean, his guy at the travel agency, to see about getting us on a flight to S.C. within the next twenty-four hours. The constant drama was taking its toll. We had just returned from another wasted trip to the post office box.

Seventy-two hours later, Dean is still "working" on the tickets.

And now Counsel announces that we really must start court because they can't keep the people here much longer (referring to the judges from S.C.).

I was feeling a bit discouraged when my daughter came by with a bouquet of Stargazer lilies and two huge "I love you" balloons. God really knows how to show up just in the nick of time. She sensed in the spirit that her mom needed that boost. After such a sweet time of fellowship and prayer with her, she invited Viv to come along with us for some lunch while Babbi was in school. Viv decline at first, saying that she thought we needed our time together. Deirdre insisted that Viv come with us instead of being home alone feeling bad because her money hadn't come. She got dressed in a flash. I could see that she was elated. We headed to Marina Del Ray, had a great lunch over looking the ocean and headed back, since it was almost time to pick Babbi up.

Viv picked Babbi up and returned appearing angry and upset. The child stood beside her looking a bit confused. She told us that a young black guy ran past her and tried to grab Babbi. She pushed Babbi behind her and was ready to do battle. She claimed that he had a cell phone, and kept running north. We called the police and they took a report. By now I am unmoved by the things that she is telling me. I chose not to engage Babbi about the incident. She didn't look like a child who had been traumatized in any way. I had my doubts about the story and figured that she had probed Babbi to lie. I didn't want the child caught in the middle. Not another word was ever mentioned about that incident.

Everything was being held up! Viv claimed that she was finally approved to get funds through DSS (Dept. of Social Services). She was to go to a nearby check-cashing place and show her ID card to get the cash. She claimed that the system kept saying "eligible", but still would not release funds. She called her worker and was told to come in and see a supervisor the following day. In the mean time the supervisor from the credit union in New York supposedly put a tracer on the check that was sent out two weeks ago. The supervisor from DSS found the problem to be that Viv needed a new card because of the funds being over $1,000. This incident botched my whole day when Viv spent four hours at DSS waiting for a supervisor that she claimed never showed up. A part of me wanted to believe her story, so I encouraged her to request a hearing. Another part of me just couldn't believe that so much resistance could be targeted towards one person. This caused me to miss a weekly scheduled ministry assignment. By now I am frustrated and too upset for my own good. Viv was venting about her troubles and whining about the changes she was going through. I realize that it was only by the grace of God that I got through any of this, because I wanted to explode!

In the interim it felt like I was watching a game of dominos. Again Viv's sugar was up over 500 and the doctor wanted to admit her to the hospital. Nothing has shown up in reference to the tracer that was put on the check from N.Y. The claim filed from the rental car accident seemed to be at a stalemate and Viv informed me that when she spoke to the claims adjuster concerning my car. She was told that Jacque gave permission to "take her time sending the funds because there was no hurry."

Viv complained to her doctor about Jacque during a visit and he offered her the name of another attorney. In the meantime, she claimed that the pastor at church also suggested an attorney that his mother knew. I didn't realize it then, but her need to change legal representation became expedient when I confronted her about never having been present when she spoke with Jacque. Although, I chose to stay in the background, it stands to reason that at some point I would be present when she spoke to him. Phone calls were inconspicuous and I was always informed later.

Viv complained that the doctor constantly pressures about going into the hospital, suggesting that I take the Power of Attorney and get things done. Her answer stayed the same. She could not go into the hospital and leave so many things undone.

Now that my mother was going to have back surgery, I needed to go to North Carolina. Before I left, Viv filled me in on the conflict occurring between Jacques and the new representation. Apparently it was revealed that Jacques had been stalling and tying up her funds from the state, as well as the Department of Social Services, the Credit union, and the claim funds from the car accident. Not that it would have taken much, but her attempt to rustle my feathers against him worked. The story goes that she called Jacques' office and was led to believe that he was in, but when she arrived she was told that he, along with Judges Lee, Lindsey and Patterson had gone to South Carolina. What a surprise! When his assistant put a call in to him, he spoke with Viv and told her that the trip had been "spare of the moment" and he would explain. Within that explanation, he supposedly said that he received word of my plans to wipe her out. Consequently, to protect her he held up the funds. I was furious! This man must be losing his mind to slander my name and think that he will get away with it. He then threatened Viv and told her that she had better count the cost before she fired him. Upon returning to L.A., he tried repeatedly to contact Viv. She refused to speak with him, saying that she believed he went to scope out her dad's land. After sharing this stressor with her doctor, he encouraged her to talk to Jacques. She did, and claimed that he apologized to her, pleaded his case and asked if they could start all over again.

Viv finally decided to take her doctor's advice and be hospitalized after her sugar reached record high's again. For the next few days I was exhausted from the overload of trying to take care of my business and hers, along with her child. On the day that she was to be discharged, I had a four-hour meeting with our accountants to go over books. When I arrived at the hospital she was lying in bed watching TV. Her excuse for not getting dressed and being ready was that she didn't know what time I was coming. I struggled to keep my cool. While she babbled on as if she were totally oblivious of my time, I had very little to say. My limits were being tested and it was best for me to keep quiet. The predicament that I found myself in was one that I would not wish on my worse enemy. Concerning this bedlam, and what I had taken upon myself, I thought of a profound statement that spoke volumes to me. I was chatting with a lady who shared how her husband had decided that he did not want to be married anymore. She was devastated, but pressed through to go on with her life. Sometime later he began to call her and beg forgiveness. He decided that he had made a mistake and indeed wanted to be married. She thought, since God gives second chances, she would give him another chance. Things went well for awhile. Then one day, the husband showed his true colors again and she began to seek God to find out where she had missed it. She said, "Father, You are the God of second chances", and I thought that I was doing the right thing by giving my husband another chance. She said God spoke to her so clearly and said, "You are not God."

Once at home Viv asked if I would pray with her. This had worked in the past when she knew that she had pushed my buttons. This time she generalized and could not tell me what we were praying about, so I rejected her request and felt not one ounce of remorse.

Even though I felt that I had reached my limit with Viv, I talked myself into hanging in there just a little longer. I had to recover our losses and I owed that much to my daughter. Had it only been myself, I would have let go a long time ago. I felt fully responsible for the way things had turned out. Of all of the creditors, my greatest remorse was for Dr. Wiley at the private school who trusted Viv because of us and still had not gotten paid for the balance of Babbi's tuition. In a couple of weeks, school would be out for the summer. Although we paid the first installment and registration fee, Dr. Wiley was still out of the greater portion of the tuition. During the time that Viv was supposedly in protective custody I would go in and share with Dr. Wiley what was going on. She had a humongous heart of compassion for children and for humankind. She allowed the child to continue her education without once ever sending a threatening letter. Viv only received the standard reminders that tuition was past due. I was deeply disturbed that she too had become victim in this charade.

Viv continued to manipulate things by flooding me with reports of her progress to produce some funds. I went along with whatever she presented, even when she told me that Jacques wanted me to prepare to be "key witness" in her case. Though I did not verbally agree, she was sure that this was another spark of interest to delay her end. She claimed to have called the credit union in N.Y. and to have spoken to the head person who told her that they were re-issuing a check immediately. The insurance agency handling my claim was to send a check as soon as Viv signed a release that was to be faxed to her. She also claimed to have called the banks in Sumpter, Kershaw, and Laurenberg, S.C. to check the status of her dad's estate. Jacques was back to being too busy and Viv refused to meet with his assistant anymore. She commented that, for some reason, Jacque was buying time. She accused him of playing games and being evasive. The promise to begin court soon was getting very old. He continued to have his assistant contact her with repetitious questions and then there was a message advising her to change her identity. This set off a spark, and when she said, "No" to Sean, she received an unexpected call from Jacque saying that he heard she was being very uncooperative. She claimed to have fired back at him that she was not a fugitive and would not change her identity. He told her that it was too late. The identities of both she and Babbi had already been changed. It had been done even before his assistant made the suggestion. She was told that she needed to come and pick up her new Social Security card and

CA driver's license and prepare to move out of my home. Jacque would see that she was escorted to the city of Puente, where she and Babbi would stay with Elizabeth, who was Judge Evan's assistant.

It is now June and according to Viv, she had spoken to the CA Bar Association, the State of CA and to all of the banks down South. From the Bar Association, she claimed to have received a lot of support after telling her story. They called the things that she reported unethical and unlawful. She was promised that it would be handled in the most judicial manner. The State of CA promised to re-issue the checks, and charge Jacque for holding the ones previously issued. The banks down South reported that all was well with her possessions. Within the next couple of days Viv informed me that she met with both the Bar Association and the State of CA in reference to Counsel and his behavior.

I could see the question in her eyes as to why this report did not phase me. Bombardments of emotions were racing within me, but fear was not one of them. Anger was in the forefront right now, and I was mostly angry with myself. Not only had I opened a door and let the fly in, but I didn't get the swat out and squash him before he laid and hatched all of those eggs.

Viv came home explaining why there was an antenna attached to the back window of my car. Someone from the Bar provided it to enhance reception on the cell phone. We were to call "911" immediately if we suspected anything. Jacque supposedly paged her non-stop for two days, until he gave up and had another of his associates contact her on my home phone and asked that she call him. He was ready to relinquish her belongings, but the Bar advised Viv to allow them to handle it. The story continues that Mother Craig called Jacques office to get a message to Viv that she should pick up her rents. She didn't want to be accused of holding them. The saga continued. Viv went to pick up the rent and was told that Mother Craig was at church. At the church, she was told that she had run an errand. The next day, Jacque called Viv again to stress that she should go and pick up her rent money. She asked me if she should go. Since this would mean borrowing my car again, my answer was…"Only if you can guarantee not to come back empty handed." She decided not to take that chance. Viv's days were numbered. She was losing ground fast and she knew it. If it weren't so pathetic, it would have been hilarious watching her simmer in her own stew. I was at the point now, where I would take the loss. I just wanted this woman out of my home and out of our lives! It wasn't long before I made that clear. I waited to see if there would be any mention about her move to Puente to stay with Elizabeth. When there wasn't, I told Viv that she would need to find someplace else for she and Babbi to stay. She said that she understood and assured me that she had already been looking. I knew that she was lying. It was obvious that she forgot what she told me about Jacque having her and Babbi escorted to Puente. I had peace and comfort in knowing that this woman was on her way out of my home, and out of my life!

I put a lot of space between Viv and me from then on. She would try to fill me in on the latest happenings, but my only answer would be silence.

In a last futile attempt she frantically knocked on my bedroom door at 4:00 a.m. one morning. Startled, I sat up in bed and answered. She came into my room hitting herself in the head with the heel of her hand and crying:" I don't want to go crazy…I don't want to go crazy". I was furious! "Then don't go crazy", I yelled! I warned her not to ever come to my room and break my rest with her nonsense again. When she kept crying and moaning, I told her that I could not help her, but I would call someone who could. I reached for the phone and dialed "911". When the operator answered I told her that I had someone in my home that appeared despondent and may be having a breakdown. Viv began begging me to cancel the call. I went into the living room to wait for the police to arrive. She followed begging and pleading with me to allow her to cancel the call. I finally agreed that if she thought her emotions were in tact, she could cancel the call. As I went back to my room, I could hear her giving the "911" operator the information.

A few days later I got home earlier than expected and before relaxing, I thought I had better check my messages. There was a message from an assistant to our pastoral staff at church. During this time the administrative head had taken a personal interest in grievances, and invited anyone who felt wronged in any way to call the office during the week. In the message, the assistant introduced herself, and without going into detail, went on to express great concern for the trouble that Viv had reported to the pastoral office. I wondered who had wronged her now. She had not told me anything about a grievance with anyone, which was unlike her. Later that evening, I mentioned the message and asked her what happened. Without even blinking, she commenced to spit out a story about someone in children's church that had offended her. The story was so shallow and weak that she trailed off midway when she saw that I wasn't buying it. I knew then that I was being set up, but I couldn't prove it. If that was not the case, I certainly did not want to make an accusation and plant another idea in that distorted mind of hers. I had been far too generous with giving her the benefit of the doubt. Nothing came of the call, but I believe that she put on her victim act and planted a seed to assassinate my character with leaders of the church.

In the midst of this bedlam, I got a call from my mom that my brother in-law was found dead in his hotel room in Philly. He and my sister lived next door to my parents. When I asked how my sister was, mom told me that she was just getting off from work and she was waiting for her to get home. Once my sister was at home and received the news we had to put her support network together. Dad would drive sis to Philly and I would meet them there in a couple of days. Mom had spinal surgery less than two weeks before, so she wouldn't be able take the drive. I had to forget about the drama that I was faced with and focus on being there for my sister. I truly did not want to leave Viv in my home. I was even advised to "clean house" before I left, but I just could not come up with a plan to successfully evict her in a couple of days. I also thought about what I might have to deal with if I didn't do things just right. She might become vindictive and I might end up on the front page of the LA Times. I mean, this is where we live. I knew now that this woman was capable of anything, and I was fed up! I spent the next couple of days secretly preparing to leave. I waited until the day before I was to leave to tell her. I did not feel good about this, but I gave it to the Lord and went on in His peace. I was blessed and grateful that my daughter worked for the airlines and that I was able to go and support my sister without difficulty. An entourage of family and friends came from different states for the memorial service, and afterwards we spent time together. I felt such freedom and peace those few days not having to contend with Viv blowing up my phone with unending drama. Undoubtedly my message was loud and clear. As relentless as she was, she finally got it... she finally backed off.

15.
Major Turn of Events

I arrived home to find everything in order. In just about a week our Summer Conservatory would be underway and my top priority was preparing the contracts for our instructors who worked during the summer. Viv was sticking close and trying to be most helpful since Babbi was still taking classes. I had placed a broad distance between us, and though it was comfortable for me, she was on pins and needles. She continued to talk about different people that she had met through the Bar Association who were willing to help her. A lady named Mrs. Smith was added to the cast of players. Mrs. Smith who was supposed to be a "big wig" at the Bar Association had told Viv that she would get her belongings in her hands within the next forty-eight to seventy-two hours. On the day that she was to pick up her package, Mrs. Smith supposedly wanted to meet her at a bank not far from the house. I was extremely busy with the details of the Summer Conservatory, being this was the first time that we would interview and hire youth through the City of Los Angeles. Viv asked if she could take my car, and I said, "No." She asked if I would take her so that she could get her things and pay us what she owed. She went on about how miserable it was to live like this and how she just wanted to get this debt resolved. Against my better judgment, I finally agreed to take her. On the way she described the woman and told me that she would be driving a blue Mercedes. The drive was about thirty minutes. I parked at the bank and she got out of the car. After a few minutes she pointed towards a car on busy Wilshire Blvd. in the midst of rush hour traffic and told me that was Mrs. Smith. I didn't see the car that she described, and her next statement was…"she didn't stop!" Displaying her infamous victim countenance, Viv went inside the bank to use the public phone. She needed to call Mrs. Smith and let her know that she just drove by their meeting place. She came back to the car with yet another story. Mrs. Smith wanted to know who "that woman" was with her. She claimed that Mrs. Smith was upset that she had not come alone. She insinuated that if I had allowed her to drive my car and meet with this woman, everything would have turned out fine, but since I was with her everything was botched. That was it! Viv figured that if she could keep this up it would buy her more time, while once again she attempts to look like the victim.

We drove back to the studio in silence. For me, this was truly the end of the road! When the day was finished at the studio, I asked Viv how close she was to getting a place to stay. She told me of a couple of places where she had applied and said that she was waiting for a call. I didn't believe anything this woman was telling me, but I was sure of one thing: She had to go! At this point I was ready to take her and her child to the nearest shelter. In fact I still had my reference lists.

Finally there were three weeks left to the Summer Conservatory and we were in rehearsals for the final production. Viv began anxiously sharing her plan. She would get her own ticket and go to South Carolina alone to get her finances. She just wanted to be relieved of the burden of debt to us. She asked if she could leave Babbi with me while she took care of business. Babbi had a significant role in the production and despite everything else, we were proud of the progress she had made and wanted her to finish. I watched and waited for Viv to put feet to her speech.

One evening, two days before her scheduled departure, she began washing clothes and packing. She was working really hard to prove to me that she meant business. She told me that "they" were accusing me of taking advantage of her, and she had defended me every step of the way. When she saw that I wasn't impressed, she took it a step further, pleading with me to go with her to the lawyer's office that had drawn up the power of attorney, so that she could obtain a "declaration" stating just the opposite of what the so-called accusers were saying. I took her up on it. Why not? I had nothing else to lose. In fact, if there was anything that would be in my favor after this nightmare, would be a legal document of this sort! Oh yes, this was something that I immediately saw the benefit in agreeing with. I realized that I had been dealing with a pathological liar and at this point I welcomed anything that would serve as a blanket of protection.

Viv continued to pack the night before her scheduled departure explaining that she had contacted the travel agent that we used when she went home with us for Christmas. She claimed that she was able to get a ticket for a little over four hundred dollars. I asked why she would spend money to travel when Deirdre could get her a ticket on the carrier that she worked for. Her excuse was that she didn't want to "bother her." She continued to pack and talk about her plans to get her monies, pay us back, and show us just how much she appreciated everything that we had done for her. When I asked what time her flight would leave the next day, she told me at 4:44 p.m. She finished packing and asked if she could put her suitcase in the trunk of my car, so that it would be one less thing to do in the morning. That would work. We had to be at the studio by 7:00 am and would not have to come back to the house. I had mixed feelings about this. I was elated that she was leaving, but did not want to get my hopes up too high. The fact that she was planning to leave was one thing, but to believe that it would actually happen was a stretch of my faith.

The next morning, we were only at the studio a couple of hours before the drama kicked in. Viv came into the office in a huff and announced that she had called the travel agent to find out what time she could pick her ticket up. The ticket price had increased another four hundred dollars. I asked why, and she told me that it was because she did not pick the ticket up within twenty-four hours. She went on a rant about the ticket agency and how she could not wait to speak with the manager, who would not be in until 1:00 p.m. I was seething inside, but I would not comment. She was looking for a bailout, but I continued to ignore her babbling until she got the message and left my office. I decided that she was going to figure this one out all by herself. I was at my end with this woman and she would be leaving my home one way or the other.

We kept our scheduled appointment with the attorney, and today, I still have a copy of that declaration in my possession. In this document, and in her own words, she stated how long she had resided with me and that she had signed a Power of Attorney, granting myself the authority to make medical and financial decisions on her behalf. She called me gracious for having chosen to divert much of my financial resources for the benefit of she and her daughter. She also stated that I had never taken advantage of her financially or otherwise, but that in fact, I had gone out of my way to accommodate she and her child during their stay in my home. She stated the estimated debt and her intent to reimburse me for all expenses. She further stated for the information of the "court" that she was never issued an order indicating that she was not of sound mind or incompetent to handle her own personal affairs, either alone, or with my assistance if needed. In summation she requested that she be given the opportunity to fully make her own decisions regarding financial issues, subject to those which she chose to defer to myself as her attorney in fact. The document was executed. Viv signed the document and we both received copies. On the way back to the studio she went on and on about how unfair the travel agency was to raise the cost of her ticket without telling her and how she could not wait to talk to the manager. Again, I did not respond.

I was not ready for the next turn of events, but boy, was I ecstatic at the outcome! I had no idea that the same day we went to the attorney would be the same day that Viv would be out of my home and life forever!

Back at the studio, it was after lunch and for the next thirty minutes the children were required to have "quiet time". During this time they relaxed on their sleeping bags or blankets and read a book or looked at a video chosen by the instructors. The older teens monitored this half-hour while the instructors took a break. I went up to my office and Viv went to make her phone call. About ten minutes later, she came back into my office spouting her anger that after speaking with the manager, he was unwilling to negotiate the ticket price. Just as she was about to go on, Dee walked into the office and heard the conversation. It was if God Himself spoke to her and in an instance she took control. She looked at Viv, and said, "Tell you what...Go down and take your suitcase out of my mom's car and put it in mine, and I suggest you do it immediately, because I have to go back to class." She followed Dee to her car and transferred the suitcase. Dee told Viv to be ready at 3:00 pm when she would leave for work and that she would "guarantee a flight out to South Carolina today!" I could see the look of disbelief on Viv's face. It hit her like a Mac truck and in that same moment, I experienced the peace of God. It felt like a ten-ton boulder had been lifted from my shoulders. I liken it to a transfer. The weight had shifted, it was all hers now, and I was free!! Even though I would still have Babbi, I knew that it was temporary, and the child was a much lighter burden.

That evening after closing shop and taking Babbi home, we were having dinner when Dee called to tell me that she had just gotten Viv on her first flight, which would take her into Charlotte, NC. I was more relaxed than I had been in a very long time, and that night my sleep was deep and sweet for the first time in a very long time.

I never expected Viv to be gone more than a few days, because the Summer Conservatory was near the end, and her child was in the final production. She pretended to be so excited about seeing Babbi perform. It was three days before I even heard from Viv and when she finally called, I was not too nice. She started right in with excuses as to why she had not called to check on her child. She claimed that the girl who was to pick her up from the airport never got there because of car trouble. I felt nothing when she told me that she had slept in the airport for the past three nights. I believe that she was flat out lying. I reminded her that I was going to visit my parents and that she needed to come and get her child. Even though I didn't say these words to her...the money was no longer an issue. All of the money in the world could not buy the peace that I was experiencing in her absence. We would recover, and because of the grace of the God I serve, I was sure of it! I asked when she expected to return and told her that we needed a contact number. I reminded her that she had not left Babbi's medical card. She was evasive concerning her whereabouts, but gave me her brother in-law's number and said that he would know how to get in touch with her. This was her sister, Danine's husband. Of course Danine was supposedly still incarcerated. As to when she would return, she was not sure, claiming there was so much to attend to. A few days later I received a letter from Viv with a return address in Sumpter, South Carolina with Babbi's medical card enclosed.

The end of the summer session had come and the production was over, but there was no sign of Viv. I hesitated to call the number that she gave me, almost fearful of what I might find out. I was beside myself that she had such audacity. After giving it more thought I decided to put my suspicions aside and make the call. A young girl answered the phone and I asked to speak with Viv. She told me that Viv had gone to a wedding with her sister. I left a message asking her to call me as soon as possible. When she called a couple of days later, it was mid-afternoon and I was headed to the studio to tidy up and close things out. I struggled to exercise the fruit of self-control. This time, I did not ask her when she would return. I told her that she had 72 hours to get her child, or I would call Mother Craig and make arrangements to take Babbi to her. She became spastic. "Please", she begged me, "don't take Babbi there." She said that she would make arrangements for Babbi to be picked up. In the meantime, I took Babbi with me to the studio. I was very tired, but my plan was to get everything done and not have to go back to the office until classes began the second week in September. I needed to rest and focus on preparing for the trip to see my parents. As I worked, Babbi was having a snack and being entertained with her favorite kiddy videos. The phone rang and to my surprised it was Viv. She had called back within a few hours. I was also surprised to learn whom she had chosen to keep Babbi. There was a couple who had their child in our program for at least two years. They were youth leaders at our church and had grown close to Dee. I had no idea that Viv had befriended this couple to that extent. She mentioned the couple's name and asked if I would pack some of Babbi's things and take her to the church. They would be waiting for me in the Youth Center. This meant coming back to the studio to finish the work on another day, but I agreed, because this also meant that I was free! I cut things short and just as we were about to leave the phone rang again. This time it was the husband of the couple who would keep Babbi. He wanted to know what was going on. He had sensed something that did not set well with him concerning Viv. I had no idea what she had told them, nor did I give it a second thought. I shared with him that Viv had left to take care of some business and that I would be leaving to visit my parents. We cut the conversation short and agreed to talk more when I saw them. On the way home, I talked to Babbi and explained where she would be going until her mom returned. She knew the couple and was fond of their daughter even though she was much older. After fixing a quick meal and feeding her, I packed enough clothes for a week, and put some snacks and drinks in her bag .Again, I was sure that Viv would be back to get her child before then.

When we arrived at the church, parents were picking up their children and the couple who was to keep Babbi was busy wrapping up. Once everything was quiet, their daughter entertained Babbi while we talked. They told me that Viv called in a panic asking if they would keep Babbi until she returned. They were concerned that she could not tell them how long that would be. I told them that I had the same concern, and would be leaving town within the next four days. I assured them that Viv was aware of this before she left. Little did I know that she had snowed the Mrs. with her lies and her victim presentation. I actually did not find this out until visiting my parents. Before I left the church that night, I gave them my parent's number in case they needed to reach me. Because the child had been in my care, I wanted to know when she was back with her mother. Usually we women pick up on things before our husbands, but this time it was just the opposite. The husband felt that something was strange, and told his wife that she needed to talk to me. He did not believe some of the things that Viv had told her.

After being with my parent's five days, I got a call from the wife letting me know that Babbi was still in their care. It was then that we had an opportunity to talk. I found out that I had been accused of taking all of Viv's income and refusing to give her money to buy even the bare essentials. This is the same story that she told me concerning Mother Craig, and I believed her. She pretended that she needed clothes and there were other things that she falsified that truly slip my mind at this time. She played the part of the ostracized victim so well that, although the Mrs. found these things hard to believe, she too was caught in that web of deception. She was lured with Viv's personal information and made to believe that only she was privy to and could be trusted with her secrets. As I thought back, I remembered the evening that Viv had come home with a bag full of outfits that were all very nice. She told me that a lady had given them to her. The Mrs. told me that she was that lady. She felt sorry for Viv and went in her closet to help fill what she believed was a dire need. Dee told me that she noticed that while Viv was waiting for her flight she made several phone calls. I found out that at least two of those calls were to the Mrs. with her sob story of needing $800.00 for the trip to go and get her monies. Of course she promised to reimburse them as soon as she returned. It happened that the husband had to be consulted before a decision was made and in the interim her flight began boarding. Saved by the plane! If it were not for the timing, they too would have been victims of her scam. They kept Babbi for five days before telling Viv that she would have to make other arrangements.

We were all unprepared for her next move. Viv had a young man come and pick Babbi up with bus tickets for the both of them. I was shocked, because I was clueless that there was a man in her life. I was told that Babbi was very comfortable with him. The couple remembered him, because he had been introduced to them as her "friend" at our spring production earlier that year; another example of her craftiness. She had been to enough of our productions to know how busy both Dee and myself were during those times. The thing about this particular show was that I was producing it, but I was also one of the main characters. My daughter had written the play with me in mind and pleaded with me over and over to play the role of the mother. I was hesitant, but finally agreed. I knew that this would mean being in rehearsals when I should be handling other aspects of the production. Thank God for competent help, but even then the pendulum still swung my way with decisions that only I could make. I found out that while I attended my brother in-law's funeral, Viv had invited her friend over to the house. She confided in the Mrs. who advised against having anyone in my home during my absence. I am not a gambler, but I would bet money that he was her "protective custody" while I kept her child, believing that her life was in danger. Amazing!

I talked to Dee nearly every day while visiting mom and dad. She was feeling the same relief. Now that this chapter of our lives was closed, we could move on and together we would make it. I totally repented to my Heavenly Father and asked His forgiveness for my failure to listen and obey. Dee was so compassionate and encouraging. She was feeling me all the way. I thank God for my children. Even though my Derek didn't know all that we had been through until much later, his love and support was so tangible.

A few days before I was to return home Dee called to let me know that she had been bringing boxes from work. On her days off she had gone by my place and began packing Viv's belongings to relieve me of the burden. She wanted to know what to do with the things, but I had not figured that out yet.

I arrived home to find six large boxes lining the long hallway that led to the bathroom, and three more in the now, unoccupied bedroom. I cannot begin to tell you what joy came over me. Dee told me that as she was packing, she felt like taking a razor and shredding each piece. We had a good laugh about it. The bible does say, "Be angry and sin not"… so we maintained order. If it were up to her, when I returned my home would be totally void of any reminders of the most recent past. I knew that if at all possible, my daughter would have relieved me of any and all visual memories.

The next morning while in prayer, I asked God to show me how to dispose of these things. I wanted them out of my home like, now!, but I also needed to do things right. I was reminded of the scripture, "Vengeance is Mine, I will repay", says the Lord. Within a few days, God answered my prayer. As I sorted through my mail I opened the bill for my car insurance. Inside was a list of discount privileges, but the one that caught my eye was for a local storage company. As I read the offer, I knew that this was the way to go. They were offering a full month for $1. I wanted to be sure that I was reading this right, so I called the toll-free number to inquire. The representative that I spoke with assured me that the promotional offer was indeed $1 for the first month, but there was a catch. The application fee would be an additional $10. What a miniscule price to pay. I was so overjoyed about having my life back that anything, yes anything….well just about anything would do. I felt like a woman who had just dropped another fifty pounds!

This particular storage franchise was quite accessible in the area, so I had no trouble finding one nearby. I called to find out their hours and give them an idea of what I would be bringing. I found that one of their smaller spaces was conducive to my need. I ran out and opened my trunk and all four doors, then came back in to begin loading. Realizing that I would need to make two trips, I decided to take the first trip that evening and I would take the balance in the morning after I finished my walk.

After loading up, I went back into the room and checked the dresser drawers to make sure that I was leaving nothing behind. I had overlooked a

drawer full of papers! I began sorting through them and my eyes fell upon a handwritten letter dated July 1999. The letter was seventeen pages long and it was from Mother Craig. I sat on the side of the bed, and as I read, my heart sank. The letter started off trying to reason with a person that was obviously beyond reasoning with. Familiar names surfaced in the letter. I knew now that at least five of the names that were mentioned as a part of the cast were real players. My heart went out to Mother Craig as she shined the light on our predator. The letter was written on yellow legal paper. Its contents were not surprising, but instead enlightening with the following information.

The names of a brother and sister (Jerry and Linda) were mentioned in an attempt to explain that there was no favoritism shown between them and Viv, even though she was manipulative and disrespectful. Apparently this woman had co-signed for Viv to get a car and she had defaulted on the agreement. Her letter stated that she had been left stranded with her credit destroyed and creditors calling her job. Her love for Christ was much of the fabric of the letter as she spoke the truth in love. She asked Viv to take all of her and Babbi's belongings and move completely, so that she could get on with her life. It pained her to have to go back on her word after having told Viv that she would always have a place in her home. Though she sincerely meant that, the drastic change in Viv forced her to withdraw the invitation. She mentioned a place called Denmark, SC and acknowledged that Viv had problems there, but she accounted it to her youth and was confident that as she grew in the Lord things would improve. To the contrary, Viv had gotten worse. She named four of her friends that Viv had meddled with and named confusion as a constant companion. She pointed out that while causing bedlam among her friends, Viv managed to keep her own friends a mystery. The names were all familiar. Viv had mentioned every one of them to me at some point. They had all played a part as either friend or foe in the charade. Mother Craig further stated that a friend had given Viv an application for a teaching position coupled with a number to call, but she never followed up. She revealed that she worked for the County and had a concern that Viv was determined to seek employment there. She asked Viv not to involve her if employed by the county because she would be unable to help her, meaning that she would not be a source of reference. The letter further revealed that on four different occasions, she ended up charging airline tickets for herself, Viv and Babbi to go "home" for Christmas. Each time, Viv "played games" up until the last minute, promising that she would take care of the tickets for her and her child, but to no avail. One trip was made without Babbi and that seemed to greatly upset Mother Craig. This is a direct quote from the letter: " We had to leave Babbi behind, which I did not like at all. All that I've told you about protecting your daughter has gone in one ear and out the other. You should have gone down town and bought you a big doll. You could dress that doll and make it look cute. You could treat it like a baby whenever you wanted, or you could treat it like a grown up. Babbi is a real person, a human being, not a doll. She is a child that needs to be raised, guided and taught the right thing. She cannot make decisions for herself. She needs a serious adult to train her so that she will make good decisions when she grows up." I could hear and relate to this woman's heart. I had been duped to believe that she was a self-centered scrooge, who only wanted to control their lives. The letter further revealed the con-artist diligently at work during their last trip.

Mother Craig wrote: "I was doubly disappointed, having no plans to go home, because I did not have the finances. You came to me and said that we could go home for Christmas, because you had saved the money. We were supposed to be on the plane at 7:00 a.m. You disappeared for the entire day and came back to the house at 10:35 p.m. with no tickets. My mother and family were looking for us. They called, asking for our flight number so that they could meet us, but I had none to give them. These things have never happened to me before. It seems that you are out to hurt me and see me lose everything."

I realized that my experience with this woman wasn't as bad as it could have been. Mother Craig had brought Viv and Babbi here, and when she talked to her about how to conduct herself in the big city, she was accused of not wanting Viv to have friends or fun. The letter made mention of two cars- a Buick, and a Ford. The Buick was in Mother Craig's name and Viv assured her that she could make the payments, because she only had one other debt. The letter revealed that she could not make the payments on the car because she was buying jewelry instead. I wondered what she did with the jewelry because she did not bring it with her when she moved in with me. I loaned her my jewelry and for her birthday before she left for her family reunion, I bought her a pair of gold hoops. She claimed to have lost them a couple of months before the end of her stay. As I was taking a pair of her shoes out of the box to reduce the bulk, I found a pawn slip. You guessed it. She had pawned those earrings. Perhaps the same was true of the jewelry that Mother Craig referred to in the letter.

As I continued to read, I tried to make sense of why or better yet, how Viv was successful at manipulating her way through obtaining two cars in such a short time. It was a two-year span between the time she arrived in LA and the time that the letter was written. The letter further stated, "I did not like the way you did the Ford, I don't transact business that way, but I wanted you to have a nice car to drive. I signed against my will. I did this from my heart to try and help you. I wanted you to be happy." She asked for forgiveness from Viv for arguing with her and vowed not to get into strife with anyone again, because of her love for God. She told Viv that she still loved her and always would, but could no longer rescue her while she went about making bad choices and blaming others for her behavior. She repented for not consulting God in the first place, and said that in everything from that day forward she would seek God first, and if He did not answer, she would do nothing. My sentiments exactly, Mother Craig!

To articulate my feelings about what I had just read, in a word... remorseful. I should have taken the time to talk to this woman. While I thought I was protecting a helpless little lamb, the wolf in sheep's clothing was gobbling us both up.

I was nearly finished cleaning out the drawer when I found a second letter from Mother Craig dated two months later. This one was two pages and she wrote on both sides of the paper. The letter began, "I am changing the locks on all doors. You have had all summer to move your things. Please use this week to get all of your and Babbi's belongings. If you don't, I will remove them myself and put them in the garage. I will give them to the Salvation Army because I will assume that you have taken what you wanted. You don't have to bother to leave the keys because they won't fit once the locks are changed. My family is concerned about me and I do not need my mother to worry. I would advise you to have your boyfriend or girlfriend put the car in their name. The first time you miss another payment or fail to pay your insurance on time, I will let them take the car. The police will find the car, so please be mature and take care of your business. Do not worry about the Buick. Just take care of your car, which includes insurance and tags paid on time. I do not feel comfortable with your friends knowing where I live, and having my phone number. I have put up a copy of every letter written to you. My family will see these letters if anything happens to me. This has been a great satanic trial, but I only fear God. God loves you and I love you."

My God! This woman feared that her safety and even her life were in jeopardy. She felt threatened and I was in denial. I can truly say that I never once felt threatened. I didn't have any dreams or visions. No angel appeared to me, I didn't get a prophetic utterance or any goose bumps. However, Holy Spirit was speaking all along, but I failed to "have ears to hear". I remembered the words of a dear minister friend with whom I had shared this nightmare. She said: "You should be dead or in an insane asylum." Yes, the adversary had set me up and his intent was to destroy me.

I sat there in a near stupor just going over the past year, and being so grateful to God for His Divine protection during a time of being spiritually deaf and blind. I recalled the times that Holy Spirit spoke to me and showed me things to which I did not heed. I was only a babe when I disobeyed His warnings years earlier concerning my marriage, but what would be my excuse now? While I am yet without excuse, His grace and mercy covered me, protected me, and brought me through. Clearly, this had been an agent sent by Satan to destroy the ministry gifts; the women, the nurturers, the passionate and the compassionate. We yearn to comfort, to take care of, to soothe, to console, and to make everything all right... easy prey to a seemingly helpless creature... "**Can the Elect be Deceived?**" My eyes had been opened to a great deal and I was grateful for the insight that I probably would never have had. One of my favorite scriptures is Romans 8:28. God's Word is true, and I believe that this has all worked together for my good, and for His glory; this test ...my testimony.

Alone with my thoughts, I started my journey to the storage center. As I drove the short distance, I remember being a little on edge as I played back scene after scene of the past year. It was over and I was elated, but I also felt quite eerie about things and how they could have turned out. Oh, do I ever praise God for His Divine protection!!

I stopped on my way and bought a lock for the storage unit. When I arrived at the storage, I was given paper work to complete and informed that I could not use my lock, but would have to buy one of theirs. This dollar storage special was really gaining interest. That was only a fleeting thought. I quickly and gladly paid the extra money for the lock and was given one of the keys that came with it. I was disappointed to find that I could not put Viv's name on the lease as owner, even though they were her things. I completed the paperwork listing myself as sole owner of the property and was shown the unit and given a gate key with the pass code.

It was two days later before I took the balance of her things to storage. It was such a relief coming into the house with nothing to contend with but my own issues. The first thing I had to do was find out where to mail the storage information so that Viv would have access to her belongings. I remembered that after she left, I received my August phone bill which had quite a few long distance calls to Sumpter and Hartsville, SC. I looked at the bill and counted seventeen long distance calls on it. There were five different numbers called between the two places. Besides two calls made to New York, the rest were to Sumpter and Hartsville, South Carolina.

I went over the bill carefully and checked how many times the same number had been called. The number that she gave me when I spoke to her did not appear on the bill. There were two numbers in Sumpter that had been called four times each within a period of six days. A number to Hartsville was called three times within two days. Viv had told me that her former pastor lived in Hartsville. I sat for awhile and pondered over the numbers on the bill, wondering which one I should call first. I put the bill away and decided to be quiet and allow my head to clear. I just needed some "me" time and I did not want to encounter any more drama just yet.

It was several days later when I looked over the bill again and chose to call the number in Hartsville. I would feel more comfortable talking to a pastor if this was the number. I dialed and waited anxiously for a voice on the other end. An answer machine came on, but I didn't care to leave a message. Being mindful of the three-hour time difference, I called the number twice again into the evening with no success.

The next morning I knew I had to try another number. The days were passing quickly, and I wanted to get the storage information mailed ASAP so that Viv would have ample time to access her belongings. I had no intentions of paying another penny towards securing her property. I chose the first number in Sumpter that appeared four times, and bingo! I didn't recognize the lady's voice, but when I said my name it was echoed with a warm, enthusiastic, "Hi, how are you?" For just a moment I was caught off guard and I guess it was obvious, because she quickly said…"this is Pam." It was Viv's friend. I had answered the phone a couple of times when she called for Viv, but we never had an extended conversation. After a brief chat I told Pam that I was calling to make sure that I had a good address for Viv so that I could send the keys to her storage space. She asked if things were okay, and I told her that frankly, Viv had not left in a favorable light. She told me that she had just seen Viv the day before and had asked about me. Viv told her that I would not want to see her. When Pam asked "Why?", Viv told her that Babbi had gotten a $10,000 contract with a major children's network and I was angry because she would not allow me to be Babbi's manager. She heard me gasp, and with a knowing in her voice she said, "That's not even true, is it?" I assured her that it was not. She said that Viv had always spoken so highly of me and that she had trouble believing what Viv told her . I explained that we had done all that we could to help Viv and were now waiting for her to take care of the business of her father's estate and get back to us so that she could settle her debt. There was a long silent pause on the other end of the phone. Then Pam asked," Did you say her father's estate?" "Yes", I answered and then went on to explain how she called me in hysterics on the morning of her father's supposed death. Pam echoed, "Her father's death...when was this?" I told her that it was in April of the previous year. "Oh my God she shrieked! That man has been dead six years!" She went on to confirm my suspicions that there was no estate. She told me that the old house he lived in had been condemned by the city within the past year and that Mr. Alston had been a taxi driver. That was the extent of his "estate."

Another myriad of emotions flooded my being. I was flabbergasted...stunned at how crafty this woman had been, and at the lengths that she had gone to accomplish her feat. I was completely dumbfounded at my own lack of perception and I felt like a dunce. Yet, I was relieved that this was finally over, even if it was at our expense. Too often I had wondered how this would turn out. At last, I had my answer!

As we continued to talk, Pam shared how she was aware that Viv had a problem, but she befriended her because many people in that town were against her. She told of how she had a reputation of fabricating the truth. Viv had even told a lie on her and it cost her friendship with someone she held dear. Pam said that after Viv left, people who had loaned her money would ask her Viv's whereabouts, because they believed that she knew. She only knew that Viv was going to Los Angeles, but had no way of contacting her. Pam explained that it was almost a year before she heard from Viv, but the people did not believe her. Then she shared something that sounded very familiar. The pastor had called her, very concerned about Viv. Apparently Viv called her former pastor (Hedges) four days before she left LA in hysterics, saying that she had been diagnosed with cancer and only had three months to live. I looked at the phone bill in my hand. Another piece of the puzzle slipped into place. Viv left LA on August 9th. On August 4th and 5th, she had called the number in Hartsville. The second call on August 5th was fifty-one minutes long. Hartsville appeared on the bill three times, so my guess is that she left messages the other two times.

Pam was not quick to believe the story and reminded Pastor Hedges of Viv's tendency to alter the truth. The pastor was convinced that there was no way this could be an act of pretence because of the way that Viv was crying. She made excuses for her and blamed the medication for causing her to be "different." I thought…"When does it end?"

The "Dragnet" theme song comes to mind, and I could insert it right here. "Another one bites the dust," another ministry gift would open her arms and her heart to be deceived. I expressed my concern for Babbi to Pam and that opened the door to even more information. Viv had told me that Babbi was an abused child that she was blessed to adopt while working for Children's services in South Carolina. She said that she knew Babbi's mother and that the child had burn marks on her body when she was released to the agency at two months old. According to Viv, Babbi's dad lived in Texas and sent child support every month. Pam said that none of it was true. Babbi was actually Viv's grandniece and her father was a "dead-beat dad" without a job, who lived from pillar to post right there in Sumpter. Viv's niece (her sister's daughter) became pregnant at the age of fourteen, and Viv having no children adopted Babbi.

As we concluded our conversation, I read the address that I had for Viv, and Pam confirmed that it was correct. She sounded very remorseful as she wished me well, and we said good-bye. I sat in silence wondering…"Would this be all, or would I get another surprise?" I had just about all I could stand for now. I realized that it was a blessing to have gotten so much information without having to probe for it. This was a woman who had only briefly spoken to me via telephone. She was Viv's friend, but she knew that Viv was dead wrong for the things that she had done. I wondered why Pam had chosen to continue being her friend, knowing that she was lethal. My grandma used to say, "A liar is a very dangerous person, because if a person will lie, he will steal, and if he will steal, he is liable to kill, because a liar will do whatever he needs to do to cover his tracks and his tail." I wondered if Pam had any concerns for her own well being. She already had knowledge of the things that I was just finding out, yet she would befriend Viv right on. Or maybe after this... she would reconsider. Who knows?

After I collected myself, I called Dee to fill her in. I think that after she got over the initial shock, she probably said something like, "Mom you are kidding me, right?" Oh, how I wished it were so. How I wished I could wake up and tell someone of this wild and crazy dream that I just had.

16.

Unforgiveness; The Bad Seed

As I pen this chapter I am preaching to myself. Even now I am having to practice what I preach. I came face to face with the reality that walking in unforgiveness is not an option. Yes, I was filled with righteous indignation, but I had to shut down my emotions and try to get past my feelings to a place where I could begin to forgive my perpetrator. Much prayer was my only resource. I remembered teaching my first full sermon in ministry school on unforgiveness. The scriptures from **Matthew. 6:14-15, Mark 11:25, 26, Luke 6:37 (NKJV)** rang in my spirit. All three scriptures (and there are many more) give clear instruction about what to do concerning forgiveness. Since God does not have any double standards and does not make suggestions concerning His statues, His standards, or His word, then there is no escape route that I can take to steer away from what He has said according to His word. I believe that our spiritual connection is somehow altered if we do not forgive others as God has forgiven us. Think about it....how can we really please God if we hold unforgiveness in our hearts towards another brother or sister? Since we have a command to forgive, but choose to disobey, how can we justify that? Praise God, my eternal destiny is not based on forgiving others, because God's pardon of sin has come by His grace established on the finished work of Jesus Christ on the cross alone, not by any man's actions. I don't believe that Jesus is referring to God's initial act of forgiveness (reconciliation) in the aforementioned scriptures, but rather the day to day cleansing of that dirty slate. The cleansing that we obtain when we confess our sins. (I John 1:9) in order to restore fellowship that gets interrupted by any sinful act that we engage in. How can I ask God for forgiveness when all the while withholding forgiveness? I believe that God forgiving me is predicated on me first forgiving you. Yes, He has already forgiven us.

That's how we got in. That's how we established citizenship in the heavenly kingdom, but when we miss the mark, when our slate gets marred we need to repent and we need His forgiveness.

As I pondered this thing, I realized that it would not happen over night, but I had to begin to deal with it or be consumed by it. I think that I would much rather be the victim of wrong doing than the perpetrator. What a cumbersome weight it must be to carry. And one must carry it until such time that they are willing to make it right.

When I was just beginning as a counselor working with the adult mentally challenged, a colleague shared this saying with me…"Unforgiveness is like acid; it destroys the container that holds it." The quote came from a speaker at a conference that he attended. He asked me if I had ever heard that. Well, up until that point I hadn't, but I never forgot it. That was over twenty years ago and its resounding truth is still a constant reminder that I don't want to be that container. Of course the acid can be other negative emotions such as anger, resentment, jealousy, bitterness, and the likes. Forgiveness is not an emotion and does not come by osmosis. It is an act of the will. We have to get past all of that negative stuff before we can even begin to learn how to forgive. I knew that I had to take inventory and at least begin working on letting go. Satan had come in one way, but he would have to flee seven ways. He had tried to destroy me and now I had to make a choice - the choice to forgive or self-destruct through unforgiveness. Knowledge is power-less unless you use it. I remembered reading medical facts about inner stress from negative emotions that suppress the immune system. Without the immune system we have no defense and we become vulnerable to every physical attack. When the acid is fed it grows and becomes a malignancy that hinders total healing. Medical science has proven that many diseases are resistant to treatment because of the bigger disease, which is the root of bitterness linked to that spirit of unforgiveness. I had to choose to forgive the one who had lied, and cheated, and schemed and manipulated me. Did I feel like it? No! But again, I could not afford to succumb to my feelings and allow them to dictate. If we gave in to every feeling we would all perish in quick sand. There are tons of things that we often don't feel like... "I don't feel like going to work, I don't feel like paying these bills, I don't feel like cooking, or exercising, or studying, or taking the kids to school, I don't even feel like praying", and the beat goes on. How many things can we honestly admit to "feeling like"? I did not *feel* like forgiving her, and in fact I did not *feel* that I was capable. The truth of the matter is, I did *feel* like retaliating. When someone has conned you and been so good at it, human nature says to get revenge.

Hindsight is always twenty-twenty. Oh, if we could turn back the hands of time.

I could see why Viv nearly had a panic attack when I threatened to call Mother Craig and take Babbi there. I wish I had called her, but I believed that I was protecting the little victim from the "big bad wolf." I was deceived and I was angry about it! I was angrier with myself than I was at my perpetrator. I lost valuable time that I could never get back; I lost money that I would never see again and more than that I had ignored the One who warned me. Dare I ask the Father to redeem the time and restore my losses?

I learned a lot about faith from my pastor, but the most prominent truth is that everything we do as believers, we do by faith including forgive. Sometimes we have to forgive in segments, a little at a time, one foot in front of the other until you arrive at the point of victory over that thing – until you can totally forgive that person and wish them no ill. The bible admonishes us not to rejoice in the calamity of those who have wronged us. "Do not rejoice when your enemy falls and do not let your heart be glad when they stumble." **Proverbs 24:17,18 (NKJV)**. That's a good one. I mean...how do you do that!? That takes a lot of faith! When someone hurts us, we want justice and we want it, like...yesterday! "Get 'em, now Lord!" I would envision myself walking into a room full of people and among those people would be Viv. I asked myself how I would treat her. Would I be able to speak to her without snarling and would I be able to look her in the eye when I spoke? Only by faith could I forgive her, because by feelings I had no desire to. In fact, by feelings I never would.

For some it is easier to forgive a wrong; for others it is a very difficult and sometimes grueling process. We must know why it is needful to forgive as well as how to forgive. You cannot do what you do not know. Besides that, we have a will and the will of man is said to be the most powerful force in the earth realm. One of the definitions of a "will" is the power of control over one's own actions or emotions. When I got saved, I knew nothing about my will. I didn't know that I had a will. In fact the only "will" I had knowledge of was the legal document. I learned that by my own volitional will I could choose to go left or right in this life; that God did not make us robots, but made us "free will" agents. He will not violate our wills and neither can we violate the will of another human. Before I had knowledge of such, my attitude in life was, "que sera sera; whatever will be, will be." According to God's Word, we are destroyed for a lack of knowledge, and because when knowledge is sent, we reject it...***Hosea. 4:6***. He has said, "I have set before you this day, life and death, blessing, and cursing: ***Choose life***." - ***Deuteronomy. 30:19b (NKJV)***.

As kids we used to play a little guessing game: One person would close both hands with a small object in one, and the person guessing would have to tap the hand believed to be holding the object. Most of the time I would tap the wrong hand and there would be nothing in it. God doesn't do us like that. He gives a choice, and then He gives a "sneak preview." He tells us which hand to tap - "***choose life***."

Unforgiveness can become a habit. Sometimes we can think that we have forgiven a wrong inflicted upon us, and be unaware that we are still harboring anger. One can put up a defense and get so comfortable in that place that any truth concerning the matter gets rejected. I did not want to be guilty of that. I knew that I would first have to acknowledge my ill feelings towards Viv, not deny them. Then I needed to pray and ask Holy Spirit to help me do this successfully. I could not do this alone. One of the main reasons why we fail to get it right in this Christian walk is that we think we can do it all by ourselves. That is just another form of deception. I have learned to call on my Help. Scripture says Holy Spirit is the Helper. The Greek word is **paraclete** or **parakletos**; one who walks along beside us to assist us, and we all need Him. God is not a frivolous God. If we could do it all by ourselves why in the world would He waste time sending Help that we do not need? I cannot tell you how many times I call on Holy Spirit - sometimes for the simplest things, such as when I have misplaced my keys or glasses. It sounds like a trivial thing, but if you have ever gotten ready to leave the house and suddenly realize you can't find those keys, you're not going anywhere. If you need your glasses for driving, you're going to have to find them before you get behind that wheel. How much more do we need Holy Spirit for those real life issues impacted by the daily choices that we make?

Forgiving is not always an easy thing, but neither is it an impossible thing. To forgive someone means to release them and all resentment towards them. I have the power to retain or release them. I relinquish my right to retaliate. The "Law of release" detaches you from the yoke of that burden. Pastor's wife used to tell us in our lady's meetings: "You can **will** to do or **will not** to do." Now, that's a very simplistic statement, but the nitty gritty of it is, your will is involved in every aspect of your life, and every decision that you make. Ultimately, you make the choice as to whether you win or lose in a situation.

I could choose to be crippled with unforgiveness crying, "Woe is me... Why did this have to happen to me? I only tried to help, and look what happened as a result." **Reality check**... Life is just not fair. Was it fair for Jesus to be beaten beyond recognition? Was it fair for Him to have be separated from God and to die on the tree for you and for me, so that we could be reconciled to The Father, and have a chance at life that we would not have without the cross? Jesus was without sin or fault, yet this was visited upon him. None of us are as good, hence the question, "Why do bad things happen to good people?" Nevertheless, Jesus forgave those who wronged Him and then He forgave me. With that in mind, I had to do some soul searching. Who was I to withhold forgiveness? You owe it to yourself to forgive. It is your healing tonic. It is for you, not for the perpetrator. We are not excusing their behavior, but simply forgiving it, moving beyond it.

This is the real deal: Unforgiveness can make us emotional cripples unable to move beyond our past, but instead remaining in bondage to spirits of anger, resentment, bitterness, and even offense. It can hinder our faith and the answers to our prayers. It can impede our spiritual progress as a child of God. How can I expect to speak to the mountains in my life and decree that they be removed unless I surrender my flesh {my emotions} to the will of God? How can I continue to grow in the things of God if I am stuck on nursing and rehearsing this thing that could become a stronghold if gave it permission? To harbor any of these negatives I would knowingly open myself up to destruction. I don't know who coined this phrase, but: "Harboring unforgiveness is like drinking poison and wishing the other person would die." Talk about deception!

Ideally…I reach out with forgiveness; the perpetrator reaches back with repentance. However, the reality is that Viv may never apologize. She may never pay her debt. She may never ask us to forgive her. That could not be my excuse for withholding forgiveness. I had to take care of my part. Whatever her choice would be between she and God. I have determined that my slate would be clean.

Biblically speaking **un**forgiveness is not a very popular word. Though my search was not exhaustive, it was extensive, and I found it intriguing that the word "**un**forgiveness does not appear in my bible, or the concordance of my bible, or the topical index, or in my Smith's Bible Dictionary, or in my Strong's Complete Dictionary of Bible Words, or even in four different translations in my possession. I found the words, *un*holy, *un*godly, *un*fruitful, *un*just, *un*righteous, *un*clean, *un*thankful, etc., but not **un**forgiveness….only the word forgiveness. I did however; find the word, **unforgiving**…..*2 Timothy 3:2-3 -(NKJV)*, pertaining to the condition of mankind's heart in the last days.

Some positive things did happen after all. The situation with my car was finally resolved after conversing with multiple claims adjusters and having the claim change hands several times. I must say, that the Durable Power of Attorney did come in handy though things were still detained. I had to fax copies of certain documents along with the Power of Attorney showing that I had legal authority to act in her stead. After faxing the requested information, I received another request asking that I mail the documents instead, because the faxed copies were not clear. A third letter followed stating that the person that hit my car had declined to purchase liability insurance. Their attempt to identify the insurance company, contact them, and verify that there was valid insurance coverage had failed. I will not rehash the details of the next four months, but I can tell you this. I sunk my teeth in, and like a Pit Bull, I did not let go until I received what rightfully belonged to me!

17.
Doing Church Just Because

Where we go to church is so important and really should not be taken lightly. The situation that I am about to share is deception on yet another level.

In 2003 my mother succumbed to ALS, (that dreadful Lou Gehrig's disease) and went to be with the Lord. I never imagined that I would end up living any place other than California. That's why… "Never, say **never**" is good advice. You may be forced to eat your own words. Three days before mother passed, she was relaxing in her recliner and called me to her side. "You're going to have to step in these great big ole' shoes until I get up from here", she whispered. Mother was six feet tall and she wore a size 12 shoe. She was trying to make me feel better by putting it that way, but she knew, and so did I that she was tired. Other statements that she made also let me know that she was ready to make her transition. I stayed on as agreed after mother's passing, to be with dad and help him out. She had always taken care of everything, so dad didn't have a clue as to how to manage the household, and didn't show any interest in wanting to know either. Don't get me wrong, he kept up with everything and knew exactly where his money was going.

My cousin Gale was working at the Marine base at Camp LeJeune and staying nearby with her mom while she and her husband were having their home completed in Virginia. She told me about a church in Jacksonville, NC about forty minutes away, that she had been attending and asked me to visit with her. Now, among my preferences in the place where I choose to worship God, I desire **teaching** among a body of Spirit-filled believers, in a non-denominational setting, and a multi-cultural congregation is a bonus. I believe the latter is what heaven will look like - people of every nation and every tongue. If nothing else, my primary preference is that the church be Spirit-filled. That is first and foremost. The church that my cousin took me to presented all of the above. The pastor taught the Word, there was an anointing on praise and worship, and on several occasions the praise team would sing in the spirit. Concerning the Gifts of the Spirit, there was a prophetic word from time to time for an individual or for the congregation. The church was non-denominational and multi-cultural. The workers were warm, friendly and professional. Expressions of love seemed to flow throughout the congregation, and things were done decently and in order. Overall I found myself enjoying the experience.

I had been going regularly for about a month when another cousin, Deidra invited me to attend Tuesday morning bible study at a church within minutes from the house. Over the Christmas holidays while on vacation, she would pick me up. On my first visit I noticed that as we were driving into the church parking lot that the words, "**Spirit-filled**" stood out boldly on the sign outside of the church. The pastor was an older Caucasian woman who presented a very warm and loving persona. She was quite jovial and made you really feel welcome. The bible study consisted of roughly twelve to fifteen people, and it was predominantly Black. Those who attended were from the nearby community and I saw a few cousins that I had not seen since my pre-teen years when we used to travel from Philly to visit my paternal grandparents.

I continued to attend the church in Jacksonville on Sundays after my cousin Gale moved to Virginia, and I attended the one nearby on Tuesday mornings. One Sunday I got a late start and instead of attending the 8:00 service in Jacksonville, I decided to attend service nearby where bible study was held. The Sunday service was very different from the Tuesday bible study. Unlike Tuesday mornings, the congregation was predominantly Caucasian and consisted largely of the pastor's family members. A member of the church and close friend of the pastor's greeted everyone as they enter the sanctuary. The atmosphere was pleasant and everyone walked about fellow-shipping before the service began I joined a few of the ladies that attended the bible study and they introduced me to some new faces. I usually look forward to the time of praise and worship, but I must admit, I was having quite a challenge receiving from this group. The worship team seemed to be in rehearsal rather than actually ministering. It was kind of a "hit and miss." One song would flow okay and the next one would be way off key. As I felt my way through this experience making mental notes and observations, I reminded myself not to judge or expect what I had become accustomed to. God had warned me years ago not to compare any church to my home church in Los Angeles. In obedience to that, I was determined that my focus and objective would be only to hear from God.

After praise and worship, we placed our offerings in the baskets on the communion table and returned to our seats. Now it was time for the Word. The pastor did some teaching and some preaching. I was okay with that as long as there was no screeching and hooping. The Word was clear and it was a good message on the promises of God, and how our tongue is the tiller and we must speak the Word mixed with faith. Every now and then she would begin speaking in tongues, and her whole body would jerk. I resolved that she was probably very sensitive to the Spirit. How else would I explain it?

A single event changed things dramatically. At the end of the service as I was leaving, the church secretary stopped me to inquire if I had ever attended a Sunday service before. I replied, "No" and agreed to fill out a visitor's card. The next Tuesday when I arrived for bible study, I received the most excited reception from the pastor. She had read my visitor's card and learned where my church membership was in Los Angeles. Wow! What a hearty welcome I received that day. She spoke very highly of my pastor and shared how they had gone to his meetings and had many of his books and teaching materials.

After bible study that day the pastor and I were talking about ministry and the likes, and I shared my background. I had been coming to the bible study two months by this time, but up until then I had not been led to share anything concerning where I was from or my ministry. Once she found out that I was licensed she said, "Sister, you're going to have to come and teach us sometimes." "That would be a blessing", was my answer. The words of my pastor sounded off in my head. "People are liable to say anything. Just take time to observe and don't be so quick to move ahead of God." I assumed the position that if it happened, it would be okay and if it didn't it would be the same. Three weeks later, I received a call from the pastor that she and her husband would need to go out of town for a few days. I was asked if I would please consider teaching Tuesday bible study in her stead. Initially I was a little surprised, but then I became excited and agreed to do it. I can't even remember what I taught on, but the people were very receptive and it was an overall blessing. As time went on I was asked to step in for the pastor on several occasions and teach on Tuesday mornings.

In the meantime, I was still attending Sunday services in Jacksonville, but things were changing there. Instead of an 8:00 and 11:00 a.m. service, the eleven o'clock service was moved to ten o'clock. I met a lot of kind people. There were multiple cell groups which met in individual homes, and did not require church membership to participate. Some of the leaders were recruiting for their groups and would invite me to join them. I didn't feel comfortable making a commitment as yet, so I just continued to observe. With the second service now starting at 10:00, the hustle and bustle to move one group out and get the other group in seemed like a cattle rush and I found myself uneasy with the change. I believe that everything happens for a reason. I later understood why I could not make a commitment to get involved, and I soon found myself making a change.

I began attending the church closer to home where I attended the Tuesday morning Bible study. Soon I was involved with teaching there on a regular basis. I had a knowing in my spirit that I was supposed to help in that ministry. While sitting at my computer one day, I heard the Spirit of the Lord speak these words, "I want my Church empowered." I knew exactly what He meant and I became excited, because I had my complete outline, and all of the things God had given me to teach on Holy Spirit. There is a saying, "When the teacher is ready, the students will appear." I was ready to go. After corporate prayer one day I shared it with the pastor. She was excited about the teaching, stating that her congregation really needed it. When she asked if I would teach about Holy Spirit at a Sunday service in a couple of weeks, I told her that I would pray about it and let her know. It sounded like a great opportunity, but in my heart of hearts I knew that I could not say "Yes". I had been studying my "would be" audience, and I knew that I would need much more than one Sunday morning to be effective with that teaching. I felt that I would do more harm than good to try and compact the enormous subject matter of God Himself in the Third Person, in a fifty minute sermon. When pastor asked the following Tuesday about my decision, I apologized and told her that I would have to decline. I could see the look of disbelief on her face as she asked me if it was the timing. I told her that it was the time element and explained what I meant. She seemed to understand and said that she would seek God concerning what to do. I personally did not pray about this again, but within a few days the pastor received a word from God that I was to teach on Holy Spirit if it took six weeks, six months or however long. I was overjoyed! Above all subject matters this was my passion and now I could be as exhaustive as I needed to be. I began preparing and Tuesday could not come fast enough! I was excited and ready to go.

As time moved on, things were going well. I had the support of the pastor and her husband. The bible study was growing. Although I could not foresee the outcome, this was one of the sweetest and most special times in ministry for me thus far. There was a fresh anointing and God's favor shone all around. I sensed a true hunger from the people who came every week without fail to hear and receive the Word of God. I learned that some of the old timers who came every week had been filled with the Spirit for years, but did not know what that really meant. They had never been taught the difference between being "born of the Spirit" (for salvation), and being "filled with the Spirit" (for power or supernatural ability). One lady in her 80's shared that she had been filled in a revival meeting about 40 years before, but she had not spoken in tongues since that time. She never knew that she could speak in her heavenly language any time she so desired. She always thought that there had to be a move of some kind, and that she had to wait for that time.

The teaching on Holy Spirit continued for twelve consecutive Tuesdays and twenty-one people were filled with Holy Spirit during that time. Although this was said to be a Spirit-filled church, up to that point there had been no teaching on Holy Spirit. I was so grateful to be able to impart what had been poured into me. I often made it a point to publicly acknowledge the pastor and extend my heartfelt appreciation for giving me the opportunity to serve the sheep that had been entrusted to her.

Several weeks into teaching the pastor asked me to think about joining the church. That would not be an easy decision to make. I would do it if I knew that it was God's will for me to sever ties with my home church and join elsewhere. I was sure that God had assigned me to help that ministry, but I was torn when it came to membership anywhere other than where I was born and raised spiritually. I remembered what brought me to this town and what God said to me so plainly. It was the fourth and final time that I had come to see about my mother. As I was packing that still small voice confirmed that I was to go and stay put this time. And then I heard the word "indefinite." That's just like God. He gives us a little glimmer, and the rest we just have to trust Him for. I knew that I would be there for awhile, but **indefinite** to me meant clearly, not permanent. Deep down inside I knew that I would be moving on at some point, so committing to membership was not something that I felt led to do.

On occasion God would speak to me concerning a specific thing that needed the pastor's attention, and sometimes there needed to be correction. Now you might be asking yourself...If this person is the pastor wouldn't God speak to them about whatever needs to be corrected? Yes,

I believe that with all of my heart, hence, my reluctance to obey God in that matter. He may have been speaking to the pastor all along, but for whatever reason correction had not been made. And because of His infinite grace and mercy, He sends warning before consequences. He will use a vessel or whatever He chooses to confirm His word. Isn't that how He does things? He speaks; we hear but fail to obey. He sends confirmation...we choose to embrace it or reject it. The first time this happened His instruction was, "You must tell them to remove the unclean thing." I was caught totally off guard. The church was facilitating a Monday night class on Care Giving for Alzheimer's, sponsored by a local hospital, and as I was about to enter the sanctuary I stumbled upon something that had no business on the church grounds. At the entrance of the church there were two tall white receptacles on either side of the front door. Both were filled with sand, and both contained a significant amount of cigarette butts. I had not seen that before. I wasn't looking for anything of the sort, but it certainly got my attention. At the end of class, my intention was to be obedient, even though it felt awkward. After all, who was I? The pastor and I were only prayer partners. I wasn't a member of her church, I wasn't an Elder, and I really did not feel that I had the authority to say anything. Nevertheless I did plan to inquire and find out why such would be permissible. The class was sizeable, and I saw that the pastor was tied up talking to one person after the other. I lingered for awhile, but it was getting late and I decided that I would address the issue when we were alone. After Friday morning prayer would be the perfect time.

I taught bible study the next morning and had just gotten home when Holy Spirit reminded me that I had not done what I was supposed to do. I had sincerely forgotten and immediately repented, "Lord, I was not being disobedient, I will do it."

I knew that the opportunity would present itself again in a few days, because It was my turn to host prayer. I waited until then, and I was not prepared for what happened. Three of us met for prayer on Friday mornings and pastor was the first to arrive. We greeted each other, and as she walked into the room, she stopped suddenly, turned to me and asked:

"Sister Nanci, what is God telling you to tell us?" I felt a sinking in my belly and for a moment I was speechless. I quickly regained my composure and finally told her what I believed the Lord had spoken to me. She seemed relieved after I told her and confessed that it was confirmation, because God had been dealing with her concerning the matter. Her reasoning was that she got tired of picking up the smoker's litter. This would not be the only time that God gave me a word for the pastor. At first there was a word now and then, but it began to happen more frequently. I became more comfortable with it, especially the times when the pastor initiated it, asking if I had something from the Lord. I was always careful to speak only that which I knew was of the Lord, and to present it with honor and respect. Each time Holy Spirit prompted me to speak; the pastor received the word and would always say that it was confirmation. She mentioned my joining the church on several other occasions. Finally one day she handed me a membership card asking me to fill it out and return it to her when I was ready. Her reason for wanting to expedite things was that they were in need of another elder on the board who would "bring something to the table." I had that feeling of being between a rock and a hard place. For the first time, I responded to her request. I explained that I was unsettled with making a decision to join at this time, but was committed to assist in any area of need. She seemed to understand my dilemma.

As I observed, I saw places where immediate change could really make the difference in this ministry. My heart was to see the necessary changes made in order for it to expand and flourish. I saw great potential and since the pastor publicly acclaimed more than once, that God had translated me all the way from California to help her in the ministry, then I would offer my input when and where it was appropriate. As God spoke, I spoke, and the pastor even made announcements from the pulpit of the changes that were coming. I wanted to see the Spirit of God move through His people and empower the church as God had spoken to me that day at my computer. The pastor would operate in the Spiritual Gifts of **word of wisdom** and **word of knowledge**. She would also **speak in tongues** but most of the congregation did not, nor were they encouraged to do so.

Many *could* be considered babes, even though they were my elders age wise, and had been in church for many, many years. Besides being complacent I observed that some came for the "fishes and the loaves", but not necessarily for the spiritual food. Donations of produce, breads and desserts were made weekly by local grocery markets, and were available for everyone. Some would come only at the end of bible study or during the week when food was distributed.

During bible study and especially while teaching on Holy Spirit I would encourage the people who had been **filled with the Spirit** to "stir up the gift", but otherwise there was no mention of it. I so desperately wanted the pastor to be the one to initiate and encourage the people to pray in their heavenly language. I felt that coming from her as a leader and their pastor she would have more influence, but it never happened. In a sense I felt that I was rowing my boat upstream. I had been warned early on. The first "Spirit filled" church that I attended had prayer teams in place at the end of each service and I shared what I knew to be my assignment with a husband and wife team. Before praying for me, they told me, "You're going to need much prayer and a covering if you are going to teach the Holy Spirit in this area." As I taught I would sense the forces of darkness diligently at work, but there were break-throughs and victories in spite of the opposition. During the teaching, one minister shared with me that her greatest challenge was unlearning some of the things that she had been taught against speaking in tongues. She had been told that she needed an interpreter anytime she spoke in tongues, therefore she felt guilty, as though she was going against God's Word if she did not have an interpreter for her prayer language. It took her quite some time to distinguish the difference between the ministry gift of **divers tongues** and her prayer language. When she finally got her break-through, she shared it with a friend, but seemed ashamed to share it with the class.

A good friend of the pastor's, who had been her prayer partner for years moved to the area and began coming to the church. She was a Spirit-filled Jewish lady with the sweetest spirit that I have ever encountered. We had heard a lot about each other through the pastor and when we met, it was as if we had known each other. She played a lap instrument called the Q-chord, which is similar to a keyboard. She loved to pray and sing in the spirit and was an asset to the ministry and joined there within a few months. She took us to a new level during praise and worship whenever she was asked to minister. God would use her in the Gifts of the Spirit and during our prayer ministry on Fridays she would have visions and we were always blessed with her free and willing spirit to share what "thus saith the Lord." During Sunday services occasionally the pastor's son and her niece moved in the gifts of divers tongues, Word of knowledge, and a few times there was exhortation. There was a sweet spirit among the congregation and except on very few occasions, I was the only speck of color present on Sundays until my cousin Deidre who initially brought me there began coming on a regular basis.

With the pastors blessing, I moved on to teach the **Fruit of the spirit**. I had held on to the membership card, and began pondering the pastor's invitation to join the church and become an elder. I really desired to be in position to help make a difference. I found out that the ministry was in its seventeenth year. I sensed a strong spirit of complacency, and by now I could plainly see that there was need of adjustments that involved discipline and order. The fact was that my home church had been a model for ministries across the nation and around the world. In my possession was quite a bit of information obtained from classes, workshops, being in the Ministry of Helps for many years and simply having been a member of my home church for over twenty years. Given opportunity, this church could benefit from that information in the areas needing change. I was confident and comfortable in my areas of ministry etiquette, and I wanted to share them and see this ministry succeed. I decided to fill out the membership card and the following Tuesday, I handed it to the pastor. It was settled in my heart. I would join to have a part in decision making and implementing change for the better in this ministry, but disconnecting from my home church I would not do. I would only be here for a season. I could still hear the word, "indefinite." I would hold on to that.

Shortly after I joined I had opportunity to see some things for the very first time which really pricked my spirit. Though the praise team had all new members now, they ministered much more often, but I noticed that my Jewish sister was asked to minister less and less. It was as though her gift was being quenched. She noticed it too, but we both firmly believed that God sent us to help the pastor in ministry. We came to realize that the name "Spirit filled" outside of the church did not reflect the internal operation. Gifts of the Spirit were taken so lightly. I encouraged her to be patient and observe. Perhaps the promised changes would be put in place. There were a few things that I found disturbing during Sunday services. The month after joining, I witnessed my first baby dedication there. The entire service was centered around the pastor's relationship with the parents of the child, and there was story after story involving the older siblings and their time of dedication. There was no teaching of the word that day.

I was not an elder yet, so rather than comment, I made a mental note. It did not end there. A certain Bible Society was invited to do their annual presentation which outlined their history and where their bibles were distributed according the distinctive colors. Good information, but there was no life in that, and again there was no teaching of the word that Sunday. I remember thinking, "what if someone came in off the streets today that desperately needed to hear from God, or to receive Jesus?" They would walk away still lost.

The day came for me to be ordained and become an elder. There were three of us being ordained, and again, the entire service was centered around the ordination which was done from a handbook. I expected to receive a "certificate of ordination" or some documentation, but it never happened, and there was no teaching of the word that day. The final thing that I will mention is what was called "Fifth Sunday." There is always a few months in the year that contain five Sundays and on "Fifth Sunday" a gospel group would be invited to sing and members of the congregation were asked to bring covered dishes. Afterwards a special offering was received for the group, then banquet tables were arranged in the sanctuary, and that was a time for fellowship and eating. Again there was no teaching of the word. The first time it happened, I had not yet joined the ministry, and I was taken aback. However when it happened a second time I knew that this was the norm. I also took note that communion was not done on a regular basis. It seemed to be an after thought or filler at times. All of these things seemed to surface after I submitted my membership to this ministry. I had seen the Bible society and the "fifth Sunday" program once before. I had not seen a baby dedication or ordination done there before I joined, so I was oblivious to the fact that there was no teaching in addition to these services, and no invitation to receive Christ at the end.

I have to admit that I reasoned in my mind about certain things being the norm because I was in the south, and "Fifth Sunday was just one of those things. I did not feel comfortable with sporadic communion and alleviating the teaching of the word. In fact, the pastor arrived at prayer service early one day, and I took the liberty to ask why communion was not offered more often. She could not seem to give me a clear or concrete answer. It was more of an excuse, which I questioned in my mind. The people's lack of interest was the blame for the decision not to have communion on a regular basis, but I was assured that, that would be among the changes.

Now we were about to have our first elder board meeting, and I knew that I needed to feel my way through this. The observations that I had made weighed heavily on my heart. I began talking to the Lord about my part in all of this. I asked the Lord to formulate and articulate the right words through me. My first elder's meeting was a bit intense. One of the elders resigned after looking the pastor in the eye and boldly declaring,... "The Titanic is sinking and you're worried about what kind of lawn furniture should go on the deck." That was pretty profound, because the gentleman, who was also her family member had spoken the truth. The weightier and more important issues were being skimmed around and over, while small talk and safe matters were brought to the table. It was no wonder that after seventeen years the ministry was not growing. God could not send increase into chaos. Reluctantly I joined in with comments and my opinion about matters that were already on the floor. Things were going in a different direction, so I did not feel led to speak about the aforementioned concerns that I had. I expected certain changes to be implemented in time, but I had to ask myself, was I expecting too much? As I said before, a spirit of complacency was evident there, and I sensed that the very thought of **change** brought the fear of losing control. I was not there to change anyone's agenda or to add my own. I just wanted to be a blessing and I was careful to make that clear.

As the days progressed, my eyes and ears were opened to some things that disturbed my spirit and caused me to cringe. I began hearing error during the sermons. Suddenly I heard scripture being taken out of context, other things were explained away, and moreover there were things that were added to scripture with the explanation that, "You have to go **deep** sometimes and not take scripture so literal." Now, I can agree with that, if we recognize the Spirit of God as the One doing the deepening and giving new facets of revelation, and not one's intellect. At one point during a sermon the pastor said…"Eve is the mother of all, and if Eve is the mother of all, then that means Eve is Adam's mother." I could not believe what I was hearing. After class as I was on my way out the pastor walked over to me and said…"Eve is Adam's mother", now sister, why haven't we seen that before?" I smiled and responded, "Probably because it does not exist." I received a pat on the arm and was told to "Pray about it." After that day I was only asked to teach once, and that was by election of the Board of Elders during "Pastor Appreciation Week."

The urgency in my spirit began to intensify. I was present physically, but withdrawn spiritually. I am pretty transparent and have never done well with pretending. My physiognomy is famous for giving me away. I am sure that my disagreement was evident, and I knew that it was time to make my exit. I was in disbelief about what was happening, but I wanted and needed to do things decently and in order. I would not allow my impulses or emotions to get in the way of doing things the right way. I prayed and asked the Lord to show me what to do and how to do it. I asked for His wisdom that I might be able to present my concerns and depart without ill feelings or remorse. I remember that my spirit was doing somersaults all the way home. I busied myself doing things around the house, and lay down to take a nap at 4:00 in the afternoon. At exactly 4:15 I woke up in frenzy. I had one of the most disturbing dreams that I have ever had in my life. In the dream, I was in a body of water and the waves were clapping all around me. The water was full of debris and the top of a small house was floating towards me. Although I was staying afloat, I was having a breathing challenge and cried out to the Lord that if He would just keep the debris from hitting me, I could make it. Just then a helicopter appeared to my left and parked on a deck that I had not seen. The pilot, a young white fellow had come to rescue me. Not realizing it, I put my left hand on the propeller which seemed to stop the minute I touched it. I was in a panic as the pilot reached for me. I grabbed a thick gold chain that he wore around his neck. As he tried to pull me up, I held on to his chain so tightly that it caused him to struggle. I heard a man just behind him, whom I never saw, yell for me to "Let go!" - Meaning let go of the chain. In a flash the pilot pulled me up on the deck. I burst into tears of joy. He asked, "How do you feel?" As I replied, "I'm ecstatic", he began laughing and tears of joy streamed down his face. I woke up to a flood of emotions and immediately grabbed my dream book beside my bed, and began writing. That dream would have great significance just a short time later.

Aside from other things, I took notice that the time once set apart for prayer seemed to have less and less importance. I was working overnight, and would get off at 9:00 a.m. and go straight to prayer. I found myself waiting from as much as ten to thirty minutes before the pastor or anyone showed up. There was seldom an apology offered, and tardiness was often dismissed with a smile, a few hugs and needless chatter. I sensed a spirit that made me uneasy, and was unable to discern what it was. In the book of I Samuel 15:22, 23 (NKJV) we read the account of the Prophet Samuel's rebuke towards Saul for disobeying God. The bible says in the first part of vs. 23 that, "Rebellion is as the sin of witchcraft and stubbornness' is as iniquity and idolatry". It was not witchcraft because I say so, but on at least two separate occasion's pastors who were invited to speak at the church were bold enough to identify and make the pastor aware of the presence of a spirit of witchcraft during the service. Another warning! The Word of the Lord had been rejected time and again. I must admit that the first time I heard it I did not grasp the depth of what was being said. However, the second time that the same warning was issued, I got it! Now I was clear on what I was seeing. When God tells us to go one way and we rebel and are determined to do just the opposite, He counts it as witchcraft.

The pastor's friend who was also the greeter on Sundays was also known to interpret dreams. She had done so once for me and seemed to be legit and right on target with her interpretation, using biblical numerology, and scripture definitions, etc. I wrote the most recent dream down and asked if she would read and interpret it, and she agreed. This time it was different. Two weeks later the church was hosting a Jewish Wedding Feast and that night, pastor's friend handed me the interpretation of my dream and said, "Let me know what you think." I slipped it in my purse and went on to enjoy the evening. I couldn't wait to get home and find out what this wild, disturbing dream could have meant. When the evening was over, I drove the short distance home with great anticipation. I got in bed, propped my pillows up, and began to read what was written on both sides of three sheets of paper. In a nutshell, this was the interpretation:

She began with numbers, definitions of certain words, and scripture. Within a few sentences I knew that I was being attacked. I had been the subject of conversation and God was no where in this interpretation. I was accused of "living under the old law, (church traditions)", and furthermore God had brought me there to sit **under** the pastor's teachings. The meaning of the old house that came towards me in the dream was "past inheritance; one's grandfather, or grandmother's religious ways or established traditions." God wanted to rescue me, but I was still holding on to some old teachings and ways that would in time choke me. I was floored when it was implied that, in my dream I appeared to be shocked that a white person would come to my rescue. The question was asked, if I had feelings of prejudice when I was younger? The interpretation further stated that in a Tsunami everything is uprooted and destroyed and God was showing me that I was holding onto some things so tight that it would take something like a Tsunami to get rid of them. Though much more was said, this will suffice.

To say that I was perplexed would be an understatement. Suddenly I was being falsely accused, I had been misunderstood, and in a word, I was flabbergasted! For a prolonged moment I became furious!! I thought...How dare this woman make such presumptions and accusations when she didn't even know me or anything about my spiritual background. I finally put my emotions in check and summonsed the Lord concerning what to do. I knew that this could not go unapprised. It should be confronted, but in His way...not mine. Determined not to be impulsive concerning this matter, I spent time with the Lord asking for His wisdom and seeking His counsel. I purposed in my heart to wait for His answer. In a couple of days I would see this woman at church. She was the one who greeted everyone as they entered the sanctuary. On Sunday I entered the sanctuary and we greeted one another, but after service she and the pastor avoided me like the plague. I remembered her words, "Let me know what you think", (concerning the interpretation) At that point, I don't believe she wanted to know what I thought. God had ordained the time, but it was not yet. The enemy had gotten his foot in the door and I had come under attack for no reason other than discerning and responding to what was blatant error!

One evening as I was waiting for the answer as to how to handle this matter, the Lord spoke to me... "You're an elder, call a meeting." Bingo! I had forgotten the pastor's announcement at the last meeting that any elder could call a meeting at anytime. I felt a weight lift. Praise God! There was my answer!

After the bible study on Tuesday morning once the pastor finished teaching, I approached her with my request for an elder's meeting. She reminded me that she had prison ministry that week, but suggested that we go ahead and meet without her. I explained that it was essential that she attend, but that there was no need for all of the elders to be present. Besides the pastor and myself, I specifically requested the presence of the church secretary, who was also her daughter-in-law, and her friend and elder; the interpreter of my dream. I realized that they were close to the pastor and I had no ally who would be physically present, but it did not matter to me. I would walk into that meeting with my Assistant, Holy Spirit, and in that I had great confidence. We set the meeting for the following Saturday when pastor would be free.

I remained prayerful that God would give me the right words to say, and that I would be able to present my concerns in an atmosphere free of animosity or offense. As I was in prayer the night before the meeting, Holy Spirit told me to write a letter. At the end of the letter, He gave me three scriptures. One for the pastor, one for me, and the last one was for the both of us. After completing the letter and reviewing it, I had such peace. He had given me the perfect words. I decided to make a copy for each person and take it to the meeting. God had heard and answered my prayer.

When I arrived at the church office on Saturday morning everyone was there. The secretary was seated at her desk, the pastor and her elder/friend sat together against one wall, and I took a seat opposite them on the other side of the small office. Everyone was cordial and I must say that I was not anxious at all. In fact I was feeling most confident and assured. I presented each one with a copy of the letter and thanked them for being there.

Once called to order, I stated my reason for requesting the meeting. I went on to read the letter aloud, which stated my reason for being at the ministry, the observations and suggestions that God had laid on my heart to share with the pastor over the past twelve months, and the implementation of change for the growth and expansion of the ministry. I left each thing open for discussion before moving on to the next item, but there were no questions or comments. By now the atmosphere had shifted and I could sense some discomfort. I prefaced the next item on the agenda with acknowledging that, while this was not an easy thing for me to confront, it was not something that I could ignore in hopes that it would go away. I shared the dream that I had, followed by reading the interpretation verbatim. In reading the interpretation, I addressed the areas that were particularly disturbing. The interpreter spoke out in defense of what she had written, declaring that she "knew what God had given her." My rebuttal was that, the **God of truth**, who knows me better than I know myself, would not have given her a falsehood concerning me. She was actually shocked to know that I had not grown up in the church at all and that my first encounter with a church after being born-again at age thirty-eight was non-denominational, and of the "faith movement." She retracted her statement and admitted that she assumed that I was from a certain denominational background. In the end, she apologized and admitted that she "may have missed it." No one else had anything to say until the end. The pastor finally said that the meeting was much needed and she was glad that we came together. She thanked me for speaking the truth in love and her final comment was: "That is how things should be approached and handled." Overall the meeting was helpful, especially to me. I found that the dream had been the catalyst in exposing a well-camouflaged agenda that was far from that which would bring glory to God. It was the vehicle by which the truth was revealed and my exodus made possible with ease. Spirit-filled...and of what spirit?

By the way, the scripture that the Lord had given for me was **Mat. 10:11-14.** (NKJV) In essence, "Shake the dust off your feet." Only my Father could be so precise.

I left the meeting feeling like I had accomplished my objective, which was to confront and resolve without malice or strife. I wasn't sure what the future might bring from all of this, but it did not take very long to find out.

In fact, the very next day in church I saw clearly that what was said at the close of the meeting was not genuine. When I walked into the sanctuary the chill in the atmosphere could not be ignored. I greeted several people as I headed to my seat, but those who attended the meeting were careful not to look my way. Though I had hoped for the best, I was not surprised. What was really in their hearts was being displayed by their actions.

I guess I'm a "die hard", because I went to bible study the following Tuesday. Somehow I was not quite settled in my heart with what I had experienced and wanted to be sure that it really was, what it was. Not only did I go back on Tuesday (glutton for punishment that I am), I went again the following Sunday with my rational being that I just wanted to make sure that this was God releasing me. Well, the final blow came from the pulpit. Without mentioning my name, the pastor's sarcastic remark was like a piercing arrow. I said to myself…"I got it…I got it now." I went home and wrote two very short letters. One was my resignation from the board of elders and the other was resigning my membership from that church. The burden had lifted and I was free!

I spent the next few months visiting churches prior to leaving for Los Angeles to attend the Annual Minister's Fellowship Convention. I remembered that the "Fellowship" had published a directory that listed all members and the location of their churches. I was able to find only one in my area, so I called to find out what time the service began. The church was small and quaint, and I enjoyed the service. However first impressions are indeed both important and lasting. There was a book written by a pastor's wife some time ago that dealt with; "How a Pastor's Wife Can Help or Hurt the Church." As a single woman, through experience I can speak to that truth. Single women in ministry sometimes catch a bad break, but that's another book. I introduced myself to the pastor and his wife as a member of the Fellowship. I felt welcomed by the pastor and others, except…need I say more?

I was determined to find a place of worship and to obey the Word of God not to forsake the assembling. The following Sunday I visited a small

"Spirit–filled" church not far from the previous one. It was multi-cultural with an anointed praise team. A friend in ministry had invited me several times and I decided to go. The church was five years old and growing. Besides the Sunday service and mid-week bible study, its outreach ministries included food, a shelter for abused women and their children, and a warehouse with furniture that was donated to those in need. The homeless and residents of other shelters were picked up in the church van and brought to church every Sunday. Sometimes you can walk into a place and it just feels like you belong. Everyone reached out to me, and I experienced the love of Christ. The atmosphere was warm and embracing. Everything about this ministry seemed to hold promise. The Word was always exciting and the pastor was also a good teacher. He had a no-nonsense quality about him, coupled with a very personable manner. The children's and youth ministries were excellent and the pastor and his wife seemed to have a genuine heart for people. In fact, the pastor shared how his wife's passion for feeding the hungry got him involved in ministry. He did not want to pastor a church, but was content helping her fulfill her mission. When he heard the Lord speak to him that he was to pastor, he "kicked against the gourd", but finally answered the call.

Most of the congregation were babes in Christ, but the pastor, along with his assistant and a few of the elder members did flow in the Gifts of the Spirit. I felt right at home. Besides all of that, he spoke very highly of my pastor and other faith teachers. My relationship with the pastor and his wife grew to be one of respect and honor. This was it. This was where I would hang my hat,…so I thought. I was elated when I was asked to teach on Holy Spirit. I was excited and could hardly wait. We conferred often as Pastor drew to the close of his series, and I prepared my message.

A few months later the bottom literally fell out. It was Mother's Day, and I thought it strange that there was no worship team in place when we entered the sanctuary. Instead the pastor chose to play a much anointed CD. I was familiar with the psalmist, who has a very distinctive voice. Once the final song had played, the pastor approached the podium and began his message with statistics. Statistics that would reveal the astronomical number of pastors and seminary or bible school students that leave the ministry each month, along with the number of churches that close each year. The information was baffling to say the least. I had no idea where he was going with the message and I was not prepared for what happened next. He told the congregation, "I only have one Leyla", referring to his wife. He went on to say that he could not be concerned about certain individuals who did not care for his wife or the way that she spoke to them or did not speak to them. He made mention of an email sent to the ministry and people wanting to be celebrated. He made it clear that no one except Jesus would be celebrated there. In a nutshell, he plainly said that all he wanted to do was teach God's Word without having to deal with the attitudes of people and the drama that comes with it. The bottom line was that there would be no worship service until further notice, but he stated that, "When we come back, things will be different." It took a minute to digest what I had just heard. I couldn't help but reflect and say to myself, "How blessed you are." **What if** your pastor who fed you spiritual meat would have thrown up his hands and quit when they talked about his wife and children, or when they spread rumors that his wife was dead while she battled cancer? **What if** he had quit when they spread lies about him personally and about his ministry? **What if** he had quit when they slandered his name and attempted to assassinate his character... when they were mean to his children? Where would you be... **What if**? It was very sobering. A deafening silence fell over the sanctuary and some began to weep. My heart went out to the young people who were just getting rooted in the things of God. I had watched young couples and single moms come with their children and babies week after week. They seemed so happy to be in a close family atmosphere. And now as I watched their faces, I could see that they were mortified. In conclusion, the pastor stated that he and his wife would remain prayerful and when it was time they would return with Sunday services. After the service I watched as people hugged each other and cried. I spoke with the pastor briefly and told him that though I was greatly disappointed, I had great expectations of them returning very soon. He just chuckled when I reminded him that if God called him, He had not changed His mind. In an article written about the ministry in one of the local newspapers, the pastor said, "I love to sing and be in the presence of the Lord, and I love the people, but I could not handle the personal issues." I prayed that his decision would be short-lived, but at the time of this writing over seven years have passed.

I continued my search for a place that I could receive spiritual edification, and be of service. One Sunday I visited a ministry that was held in a huge warehouse. I had heard that there were three services on Sundays, so I decided to go to the middle one that began at 10:00 am. As I arrived, the first service was letting out, and there were several men directing the traffic which let out onto a major road. The parking lot was packed with cars and people scurrying to their cars as they left the first service. I was finally directed to a space on a small hill beneath a tree. I made my way into the building through a very large foyer where greeters with big smiles welcomed me. As I entered what seemed to be the sanctuary, which looked as though it seated at least 1,000 people. I later learned that the seating capacity was 1,500. There were three sections with wide aisles, and the walk was long and on a downward slope. I'm short, and I have never liked sitting in the back, so I made my way down to find a seat near the front, which was already pretty full. All the way down the aisle I could see coffee cups on the floor beneath the seats. I thought...."what a mess to have to clean up between each service." Wow...I had never seen a church service so liberal. I found a seat on the fourth row from the front, and observed the service. The music was loud and more like rock. The young pastor was engaging, and had an appealing message. He reminded me of a motivational speaker.

He did not use a bible, and I'm not so sure that he even quoted a scripture. After his message, he invited a young lady to the platform to sit in a talk show style format and share her testimony. The most disturbing part of this experience was the absence of an invitation for salvation. The opportunity to receive Jesus as Savior and Lord was never given. The congregation was dismissed after information was given about the plan to add a fourth service. We were asked to stop at computers stations in the foyer where laptops were made available to take a survey choosing one of the time slots. The "gospel of accommodation" had just became extremely clear to me. Although we were asked to choose a preference to an added service, I listened to a pastor who took it a step further in describing this "gospel of accommodation." In his research he discovered that many of these ministries are propagated by young, bright, talented ministers who have comprised a formula wherein they go into the communities with their leaders and take polls to find out why people don't attend church, and what would make them change their minds. What would they like to see, what would they like to change? Make everything comfortable, convenient, and seeker friendly. Appease and satisfy the flesh. Conform to the desires of men, and in the process deceive even the elect of God after designing their own gospel. These are becoming some of our mega churches, and they are blossoming and flourishing above and beyond all religious movements in America. They are acceptable to those with "itchy ears" and carnal minds, who are comfortable being "luke warm." It doesn't cost them anything. They do not have to make any adjustments to their lifestyles, they do not have to die to self. Anyone and everyone is welcomed, and they never have to worry about being confronted in their sins. Jesus was confrontational. He was serious about the reason that He came... "***to seek and to save that which was lost***."... ***Luke 19:10 (NKJV)***

God by His Spirit will call you out! Not by your name, but you will know for sure that he is talking through the ministry gift to you. Not to harm you, but because He loves you and because he wants to help you.

I began going regularly to another "Spirit-filled" church that I had visited during the time of my searching. An evangelist friend and her husband made the same choice and before long, I began seeing some familiar young couples and their families.

I attended the church regularly for well over a year before changes that interfered with order made it difficult for me to stay. The pastor and founder of the church was stepping into his call as "Apostle", and his son would be the new pastor. I thought that was a good thing. The same was taking place at my home church in Los Angeles. The Gifts of the Spirit were in operation from time to time. There were two in-house prophets and a prophetess who would give a word for the congregation most of the time and once in awhile a personal prophecy was given to leadership. One Sunday the young pastor felt led to give an invitation at the beginning of service for those with a desire to be filled with Holy Spirit. He asked those of us who were already filled with the Spirit to pray in tongues as he ministered. With over ninety respondents to the invitation, the staff was not sufficient to handle the numbers. Praise God that some were filled and did speak in their heavenly language. However, most of those who lifted their hands to receive Holy Spirit left the alter confused and with a lack of understanding. I could read some of their faces and see the questions. It saddened me and my heart was heavy. I wanted to pick up where the pastor had left off. Maybe take them to another room with the rest of those who had assisted him and at least give the biblical explanation of what they had just experienced and perhaps what they should expect. I was disappointed that there was no follow-up or teaching, and as a result Christians often go away ignorant of the Word and confused, giving the enemy a gateway to continue to divide and conquer. I never witnessed another invitation offered there to be filled with Holy Spirit. The young pastor began to put gimmicks in place, and to go after numbers, and worldly ideas and ideals. The congregation began to dwindle, and before long the regulars were not coming anymore.

We know that many churches go through this phase when there is a change in leadership or some other adjustment that is unfamiliar to parishioners, but this was different. The young pastor seemed to be working hard to appease the masses rather than allow the anointing to flow, and the Spirit to do the drawing.

"We are to earnestly desire the best gifts."

I Corinthians 12: 31 (NKJV)

Whatever the best gift is for that moment or for that hour - whether it be the interpretation of tongues, a word of wisdom, gifts of healings, or any other spiritual gift mentioned in chapter ***12: 8-10***. When we pray and earnestly desire these Spiritual gifts, they will manifest by the Spirit of the Living God to meet the needs of His people. I matriculated through four supposedly "spirit-filled" churches within seven years. Not once did I hear a prayer along the lines of, or any indication from leaders desiring the best Gifts of the Spirit to be in operation among the assembly. I also do not believe that God has any new methods of saving folk. He did not come into the disco and get me. When I was ready, I came to Jesus. In my opinion, manipulative gimmicks designed to attract young people or certain crowds have no place in the church. One of the most distracting and annoying things that I experienced there was strobe lights during worship and praise. They would pan the congregation in bright multi-colors that whipped back and forth in crisscross motion, blinding you on the way. Someone must have complained, because after a couple of weeks the strobe lights were confined to the platform and ceilings only. The gimmicks continued, and at one point we were invited to help ourselves to the popcorn, which was lined up in containers on tables in the main foyer. "Just grab your popcorn on the way in>" The series was called, "At the movies." A few weeks later there was coffee set up on banquet tables as you entered the foyer on your way into the sanctuary. I had a flashback that morning, and then I remembered how this young pastor shared that he has visited and spent time with the pastor who has the huge warehouse ministry. It became obvious to me that he thought incorporating liberal practices from another ministry could be impressive and even work to grow this ministry. The walls on the platform were suddenly painted black and some of the young worship leaders donned and displayed their bare arms with graphic satanic tattoos, i.e., dragons, serpents, skulls, and bones. The coming attraction announced by the young pastor was that cell phones would be allowed during service with the invitation to text the pastor with any questions pertaining to the lesson. Though he would have inspiring messages, the good solid teaching was absent. I stayed at that church as long as I could stand to, which was probably too long. Once I stopped attending, I decided that I would just be still for awhile. I looked forward to the following month because I would be in Los Angeles. It was time to attend the minister's conference again. I would get my spiritual tank full and return with nuggets to share in my weekly bible class.

When I did return to North Carolina a light bulb came on. I found out how to stream live and tune in to enjoy service with my home church in Los Angeles via the Internet every Sunday. I wondered why I never thought of that before now. No, I was not assembling with the saints of like-precious faith at this time, but I was content in my heart. Sometimes you've got to do what you've got to do and make the best of it for the time being. I could not and would not go backwards. Sadly, but not surprisingly, a few years later, this ministry after twenty plus years was forced to close its doors.

18.

SEE-ming Appealing Can Be De-SEE-ving

Lots of times what we "see" is not what it is. Finally I am led to deal with what I count as one of the utmost despicable forms of deception. For the world to embrace and celebrate every lust of the flesh and of the eyes is to be expected. However, when a Christian follows after this pattern, the bible says we have chosen to make God our enemy.

And so it is when a person decides to become involved in a heterosexual relationship with no intentions of being true to that relationship. Their involvement in the relationship is void of truth and is strategic, serving only to masquerade, to cover and to satisfy their own self-centered, self-serving agenda, while their prey is set up for deception and destruction. Two real life situations come to mind, in which I was privy to the details and given permission to share them. To be specific and explicit, I am referring to a man who has a wife, and becomes deliberately sexually involved with another man…which is known as the "down low"; an accurate title for this heinous behavior.

"Now the Spirit expressly says that in latter times some will depart from the faith, giving heed to deceiving spirits and doctrines of demons, speaking lies in hypocrisy, having their own conscience seared with a hot iron."

Timothy 4:1-2

I remember watching a very popular talk show back in the 90's. The host interviewed three transvestites who were a part of the stage production, "La Cage Au Faux", and looked like carbon copies of three very beautiful entertainers. As they were asked about their relationships with men, each one testified that their clientele was approximately ninety percent married men. I was floored, but at that time I had no knowledge of the term "down low" and what it meant. I actually got a full understanding years later in the form of a movie that was sent to me. My niece, Marsha called and told me that she had mailed a surprise for me. When I received the package there was a movie inside. I had no idea what I was about to see. The first surprise was that two people whom I knew very well were cast in the movie. I thought that was the only surprise, however. As I continued to watch, the content of the movie took the word, "**surprise**" to another level for me.

A wealthy businessman and his wife offer an old school mate, who is a successful psychiatrist, a home, a hefty salary and other enticing luxuries to move his family and practice from Atlanta to New York City. After the move, an unforeseen cut in salary causes a slight rift in the friendship. Then the good news of recovery coupled with significant increase and an upgrade in living quarters, patches everything except the marriage relationship. Once the excitement of moving into their gorgeous new home subsides, the wife of the psychiatrist is noticing a change in her husband that she can't pinpoint. During times of intimacy he is too preoccupied to participate. At one point He asked her, "What if I'm not the man that you think I am?" Her answer is a quizzical look, and then she dismisses the question. She is a Christian woman who loves the Lord, loves her family and cannot wait to find a place of worship. She soon finds a church through a close friend who happens to live in the city. Hubby goes along, but when it is time to join, he hangs back. His only explanation is that, he "just can't commit right now." She is invited to the women's group at the church, which she finds interesting and regularly attends. The topic of discussion happens to be, "Dealing with infidelity in your marriage." Everyone in the group is pretty vocal except a little lady whom everyone else deems strange. She sits alone and never says a word. She would be the key to an eye opening traumatic reality in the world of an innocent God-fearing woman, who by her own admission "saved herself for her husband."

The businessman and his wife have an "arranged marriage." She is painfully aware of her husband's "sleeping around" with his male lovers and has "bitten off more than she can chew." She begs him to understand that she wants a normal life and children. He pleads just as hard with her to understand that he just can't do this "normal thing." She tries to drown her agony in alcohol and the abuse of prescription drugs, and it is clear that she is losing her mind when she walks in front of an oncoming truck in an attempt to end it all. Besides being one of her husband's lovers, the new psychiatrist in town is also her therapist. She becomes clutchy, obsessive and out of control to the point that the wife of the psychiatrist is convinced that she is having an affair with her husband. In reality her husband is involved in a love triangle with the businessman and a well-known entertainer. The entertainer also happens to be the husband of the strange woman who sits alone in the women's meetings. She is also the one who finally tips off the psychiatrist's wife, who then goes to a hotel where she finds her husband and the entertainer compromisingly engaged. The woman is devastated, to say the very least. In a confrontation just before leaving him, she asked her husband one question… "Did you use protection?" He answered, "No." Towards the end of the movie, the husband meets with the pastor and during their conversation the pastor makes this profound statement. He said, "It is cruel and selfish to bring a possible death sentence to those that you say you love, for a few selfish moments of lust and pleasure."

I shared this movie with a friend, and after watching it she revealed the pain and anger that still surfaced for her after over twenty years of being divorced. She sat down and told me her story. Artra met her ex-husband at a boat show when he visited her hometown in Detroit. Sonny professed to be a Christian man, and after dating long distance for nearly a year, she fell in love with him. He asked her to marry him and move with her daughter to his home in Sacramento. It was at a time in her life when she was searching for more of God and did not know where to find that fulfillment. She enjoyed watching a pastor via television and before they were married, she asked her fiancé to visit that church, since it was near him. She thought it might be the perfect place to attend once they were married. After honoring her request he assured her that she would like the church. The wedding was to be held in her hometown and one day while making preparations, Artra asked her mother and a close friend if they sensed anything that was not right. Her mother said "No", and her friend told her that she was too suspicious. Deep inside Artra had a feeling that something could be off, but did not have a clue what. She admitted that she did not know then, but later learned that it was Holy Spirit, who shows us things to come. He was warning her just as He was warning me, and just as He will warn you. It was less than two years after they were married and had moved to Sacramento that she began seeing a change in Sonny. He would often visit the home of a gay friend where a lot of married men hung out. Artra thought little of it at the time, because the host, J.D., was a very personable guy who loved to cook and entertain. Besides, all of the men were married and just hung out to watch sports and enjoy a smorgasbord of good food, or so it seemed.

She began to observe an element of competition with Sonny, especially when they would get dressed to go out. There was a display of child-like behavior coupled with being critical of everything that she did. He needed approval and praise daily. Verbal abuse, lying, blame and manipulation began to surface. He would accuse Artra of her female friends and constantly found fault with her child. At her mother's request, Artra sent her daughter back home in hopes that she and Sonny could work things out.

Artra learned that her husband's family was in total disharmony, and that he had a deep-seeded hate for his brother. She later learned that his brother had molested him from the ages of five through twelve. Things in the marriage did not change, and as a result of stress she suffered continual outbreaks of skin lesions, fell into a deep depression and decided to seek counseling. After a few sessions, she told the therapist that she felt an urgency to leave her husband. The therapist arranged a session with Sonny, and would later tell Artra that he was not a good candidate for marriage. When she asked why, the therapist would not divulge the reason. She knew then that there was something deeper than her eyes could see. One night as she lie quiet, waiting on the Lord for answers He showed her what she had been up against in the form of a spirit that she could not clearly discern.

A month later as Artra was vacuuming the apartment, she decided to get into every nook and cranny. In doing so, she got on her knees, and pulled out two pairs of Sonny's shoes, and a pair of sneakers that he seldom wore anymore from beneath their bed. Once she was finished and was about to place the shoes back under the bed, she saw something white stuffed down towards the toe of one of the sneakers. Her first thought was that it was a sock that didn't make it to the wash. As she reached for it, she realized that it was not a sock at all. She found a two-page hand-written letter from one of the guys who frequented J.D.'s. The letter was addressed to Sonny, and the question was asked…"When are you going to stop dragging your feet and tell your wife about us? Stop prolonging this. It only makes it harder for everyone concerned. Are you going to tell her or do you want me to do it?" Clearly this was the reason for the therapist's comment, and this was the reason for the urgency that she felt to leave her husband. A sudden rush of nausea hit her and she barely made it to the commode. After collecting herself, she sat quietly in a near stupor and began piecing things together. It was all coming together now…it was all making sense. She pondered the details over and over before deciding not to confront Sonny, but to keep what she had learned to herself. She would spare herself the lies and excuses, and verbal abuse that she knew would come from him. She had all of the evidence that she needed to make her next move. She saw her husband for the person that he truly was, the one who had come to deceive her.

Satan has no new tricks, just new characters through which to work his tricks.

Sherry, who was a nineteen-year-old college student, recently had her heart {figuratively} ripped right out of her chest. She met Syd at church, and they hit it off famously. Her parents were so pleased that she had at last become attracted to a Christian fellow. They became good friends and her parents were very fond of Syd. After dating for nearly a year, they had gone Christmas shopping together and were making plans for the holiday season. On Christmas night, after a full day and a great dinner at the home of her parents, they went for a drive. In Sherry's mind, she believed that Syd was as serious about her as she was about him. She fully expected him to pop the question,...if not then, someday soon. Instead, he dropped a bomb. Syd told her that he had decided to go back to his old boyfriend. At first she thought that she wasn't hearing him correctly, or that this was one of Syd's jokes. He went on to explain that he had been in this relationship prior to meeting her, and that he and his friend recently realized that they want to be together. Sherry was floored, to say the least. She had flashbacks of the times they had been intimate without ever using protection. A knot formed in her stomach, and a thousand "what ifs" flooded her mind. Now she fears that her life could be in danger because of his choice to use her as his mask. Sherry grew numb from the information that she had just received. Her mind was bombarded with conflicting thoughts and questions. It was exceedingly difficult to process what she had just heard. It was bad enough that Syd was breaking off with her, but to turn his affections towards another guy was devastating. She felt embarrassed and worthless. Syd had dumped her, and her competition was another guy? Why did he wait until now to tell her? What would she tell her parents and friends? For Sherry it had been the most wonderful time of the year, until she was hit with this ugly ungodly news. She truly loved Syd and believed that he was telling the truth when he told her that he loved her. What about their friendship and all of the great times that they shared? It had meant the world to Sherry, yet it was just an insignificant pass-time for Syd. Sherry withdrew from everyone and everything.

Besides her aunt, who shared this story with me, she never told anyone the truth about what happened.

The bible reveals a multitude of ways that deception will come. I am reminded of Solomon and how God blessed him with great wealth and wisdom, but his love for many foreign women and their gods and goddesses caused his heart to turn away from the God of Israel. Because deception was given free reign, he was ultimately destroyed. Deception can and will come through offense, communication, pride, philosophy, riches, loved ones, friends, and those who have been planted by Satan in the crossroads of our lives. Jesus, Himself warns us that false prophets will rise up and deceive many. We are to be on the alert!

"Be sober, be vigilant; because your adversary the devil walks about like a roaring lion, seeking whom he may devour".

I Peter 5:8

Even though there is an element of good in the some of things that I am about to mention, there is still a need to be informed, to be mindful, and to be prayerful concerning the following....Some of the music that we listen to, and especially what we allow our children to listen to; the shows that are televised with super-hype and such a captivating draw (even cartoons); some of the clothing and the jewelry that we wear, even some selections of crosses that are worn by Christians; the myriad of games that have swarmed the market and end up in our homes making junkies not only out of our children, but of many adults; some of the artifacts that we collect unaware of their origin. Some derive from different cultures that are known for delving in witchcraft, voodoo, and the occult. These items are colorful, they are mystical, and attractive to the eye as they hang on our walls and are sprinkled throughout our homes as décor. Of course we cannot negate the internet and other forms of technology that infiltrate our daily lives with such demonic subtleties. The very nature of many of these things is **deception**.

A perfect example of opening a door for spirits of demonic nature to enter and wreak havoc, is a movie that was very popular in the 70's; The Exorcist. In it a child was innocently introduced to a Ouija board, and consequently was demonically possessed. Ouija boards were once, and possibly still are sold amongst toys. In fact when I was fifteen years old, my mother bought a Ouija board for us one Christmas in the toy department of a major department store. Of course we all thought it was really cool, and tried to work up the magic of it unaware of its origin. The Ouija board, also known as the spirit board or the talking board was created in 1890, and was purportedly used in seances by spiritualist to communicate with the dead. This is a great example of being ignorant of the origins or intent of things that we bring into our homes. My mother had no earthly idea what she was introducing to her family. After all, it was found in the toy department. What possible harm could it bring?

In these last days some tricks are coming down the pike that we will not have seen the likes of. Remember that Satan is an impostor, and his imitation has to be so close to the "real deal" that it is near impossible to detect the difference. He also gives gifts, and uses deceptive ways that look like God is blessing you. In fact, you may even call it a blessing. Receiving stolen goods from someone at a "discount" price is not a blessing. The enemy is setting you up. Know this… if an evil or immoral act is attached to a "so called" blessing it is not from God! If sorrow follows in any form – It is not God! God adds no sorrow to His blessing. Prov.10:22 (AMP.)

We will see an epidemic outbreak of deception in the world. The world has no ability to ward off the attack or resist deception, but what a tragedy when the Church becomes infected with this insidious disease that oozes deadly venom.

The following scriptures sum it up...

"But know this, that in the last days perilous times will come: For men will be lovers of themselves, lovers of money, boasters, proud, blasphemers, disobedient to parents, unthankful, unholy, unloving, unforgiving, slanderers, without self-control, brutal, despisers of good, traitors, headstrong, haughty, lovers of pleasure rather than lovers of God, having a form of godliness, but denying its power. From such people turn away!"

2 Tim. 3:1-5 (NKJV)

"But evil men and impostors will grow worse, deceiving and being deceived."

---

2 Timothy 3:13

I stand in amazement at some of the things that are being welcomed, and accepted in many churches as extracurricular activities. Churches that are dabbling in the occult seem to be totally oblivious. I will begin with yoga, which has its place, but the church of the Lord Jesus Christ is not that place! Statistics report that 36 million Americans are practicing yoga, and it is a 10 billion dollar industry! I was shocked to find that the largest missionary organization in the world is not Christian, but Hindu. Their gurus come to America specifically to evangelize and win converts. The disheartening thing is that they have been very successful. To quote a speaker from a "World Congress on Hinduism" convention held in 1979 and attended by 60,000 delegates...."Our mission in the West has been crowned with fantastic success. Hinduism is becoming the dominant world religion and the end of Christianity has come." It has been a subtle deceptive integration, and if the Church does not wake up, it will be an aggressive takeover.

When I think about it, the YMCA was among the first of organizations to introduce and promote yoga. YMCA is the acronym for "Young Men's **Christian** Association." I have never had a desire to practiced yoga, but I remember when I first heard of it in the 70's. I was coming out of my theatre class, and there on the marquis of the YMCA across the street was an invitation to come in and try yoga. I wasn't a Christian at that time, but for whatever reason, I was never even curious. Because of its origin (Hinduism), Christians should refrain from any involvement in this practice. Yoga has become so popular that some churches are offering "Christian yoga." Christian yoga classes, and yoga centers that offer bible studies are on the rise. Christian Yoga is an oxymoron. Yoga is a Middle eastern practice rooted in Hinduism, and the truth is that celebrated Hindu authorities declare that it cannot be separated from its origin. I am aware that there are different types of yoga, however Hatha is the branch of yoga that appears to be the most popular form in Western culture. Sure, yoga is promoted as being good for your physical and mental health, and spiritual well being, but with the practice of yoga, know that you are allowing yourself to become a portal; an entryway for demonic activity in your life. Those who believe that they can circumvent the system by saying, "Oh, I only practice yoga for the moves and the stretches", are deceiving themselves. If you are participating at any level, you set yourself up for a fall. You see, the subtle transference of spirits await your invitation. The devil just wants access, and the yoga postures and breathing techniques that usher one into meditation, gives him that access. I like an analogy that my pastor often used. He would say, "You can't ask for a glass of water in a restaurant, and say... Hold the wet." No, the wet comes with the water, so does the malevolent spirits with the practice of yoga.

Yoga was designed, and is still used to awaken the kundalini; a dormant and serpent-like spirit coiled at the base of the spine (the tailbone). Through yoga meditation, coupled with the moves and the chants, the kundalinic force is first awakened, then travels up the spine to the chakras, which is basically described as your psychic energy centers. There is said to be seven chakras altogether. Six, plus the crown chakra. When you practice yoga you are harnessing and channeling the power of the kundalini spirit as it travels up hill to different parts of the body; each aligned to an individual chakra. Once the sixth chakra, called the third eye (located between the eye brows) is engaged, you are now beyond the physical elements, and have entered the gate of higher consciousness, which some also call God-consciousness. Within the different types of yoga, Mantra yoga is said to be so seductive and generates such a powerful supernatural experience that it makes you feel that you have arrived and are actually encountering God. Since Satan masquerades as an angel of light, would he dare to pretend to be God? You bet he would!. The moment that he has any success with that manner of deception, what a victory for him! What joy he would have in keeping that ball rolling as he tricked one after the other into believing that on their own, they have reached the ultimate plateau and are really having authentic encounters with God. Well this just blows a hole in Jesus' claim,

---

"I am the Way, the truth, and the life. No one comes to the Father except through Me."

John 14:6

Why would I need Jesus? If I can go straight to God through meditation, then I have just proved that the words of Jesus are a falsehood. You can see the deception of the enemy so clearly. He has successfully convinced you that to be in the presence of God you don't need a mediator.

I have heard some bone-chilling stories, which resulted in amazing testimonies. One young lady shared that while practicing yoga, she engaged the third eye and began to levitate and have out of body experiences wherein she could actually look down and see her body. She thought that she was dying, and began to fight with all of her might to snap out of that terrifying experience. Another lady had a like experience, but only she began to have psychotic episodes. She said that she was told by her guru not to worry, but be patient, because she had finally arrived in that place of God-consciousness, but that she was experiencing was the purging process of her karma. She became deathly ill, and her parents shaken by the state that she was in sought medical help from many doctors, but none could find the root of her problem. The next step for her was a mental institution. She decided that committing suicide was the only way to end this torture, but prior to following through with her plan, she cried out to God and asked Him to show her that He is real. Then she encountered Jesus! Hallelujah!! It is a great thing when people who were once ensnared by the enemy can share their testimonies, but it is of greater significance and much more important that our spiritual leaders in the local churches who have been given charge over the sheep, begin exposing the works of darkness so that God's people are equipped with knowledge and truth.

Now, scripture does say that the time is coming whereas they will turn away from sound doctrine, wanting to have their ears tickled, they will seek after teachers who will satisfy those desires, BUT…Nevertheless, the doctrine of the Lord Jesus Christ must not be watered down or compromised in any way to accommodate these carnal desires.

Christians should also know that astrological signs is not who they are. Be careful what you speak of yourself. Be mindful of what you call yourself, and what you allow others to call you. For example: The person who ascribes to the zodiac sign "Gemini" may think that it's all about "standing out" and having fun, even to the point of being proud to be called the "Twins." Think of what that sign represents. Implicated within are two separate people, further implied is a split or multiple personality. I think of Dr. Jekyll/ Mr. Hyde. I ultimately come to the double-minded man that the bible speaks of in *James 1:8*. Satan wants your mind. This may seem a little extreme to some, but there's a mental disorder called bipolar disorder. One of the clinical terms is manic depressive disorder. This is all representative of the zodiac sign Gemini. I used that example because this was the end result for someone that I know personally. The choice is not easy when you either have to take psycho-trophic drugs to manage the behavioral episodes or fight your demons on your own never knowing which ones will show up on any given day.

When I was a babe in Christ I had a bible teacher who was bold with the truth. One night as she was teaching she began talking about how we as Christians identify with the signs of the zodiac, and she used an example that rocked me. She said, "You call yourself a Cancer, and then when you get cancer, you don't make the correlation; you wonder....What happened?" That was profound! I was still buying the daily newspaper to read my horoscope so that I could have some assurance about my day, my future and what it held for me. She went on to say that our God is not so limited that He has to group all of His children into twelve astrological signs in order for us to be unique. I was still trying to connect with the supernatural, although I was not aware that I was doing it. Within a few weeks time, God brought the message to me again. This time my pastor was teaching, and he told the story of how he and his wife went to a Jim Jones meeting one night, because he was still searching for something more, something deep, something "spiritual." In the context of his message, he warned us ladies to be careful, because we are naturally drawn to spiritual things, whether they be good or evil. Then he talked about how we get caught up with the occult through astrology, and how it is an open door for the enemy to come in and bring destruction. For me that was God confirming His word in my life. I never again read another horoscope. If you are a Christian, your only sign should be "The sign of the Cross."

Much later in my walk with the Lord, He confirmed what my bible teacher said by reminding me that out of the billions of people on this planet, He created us so uniquely that there is no duplication of fingerprints, there is no duplication of DNA (except that identical twins are said to have the same DNA profile). To be clumped together with a million other people under a said astrological sign falls somewhat short of unique.

We must realize that everything God made has been perverted by the evil one.

Astrology is a perversion of Astronomy. Astrology is a pseudoscience, in which there is a system of methods and theories based on the assumption that the position of the moon, sun, and stars affect human affairs, and that one can foretell the future by studying the stars. In this group are witches, wizards, and familiar spirits.

Astronomy on the other hand, is the science of the universe (to know the times and the seasons); the study of the galaxies, stars, planets, their origin, composition, motions and sizes. Astronomy pointed us to the Star of Bethlehem. That star led the wise men to Jesus...."and behold, the star which they had seen in the East went before them, till it came and stood over where the young Child was." **Mat. 2:9 (NKJV)**

I am blessed to have come through an era when these things were gaining popularity, unscathed, and I am sounding the alarm! I am guilty of being curios about the occult. I would faithfully go to my favorite occult shop every month when I lived in Philly to make sure that I got my monthly scroll, which had the zodiac sign with its signet beneath. It was impressive. The enemy is so crafty. The scroll was written calligraphy style on what looked and felt like parchment paper. I did not know this then, but when I think about it, that was another guise of perversion. After all, wasn't the original script of the bible written on parchment paper?

I have had the tea leaves reading, the crystal ball reading, and the tarot card reading. I would buy and burn the candles of several different colors; each color representing a different promise; Love, Health, Prosperity, Happiness,Peace, etc. I remember being twenty-one years old when I had my palms read. The old man lived down the street from a friend that I often visited, and he had the love and respect of everyone in the neighborhood. I was curios, and decided that I wanted to see what he had to say about my life, so I asked him and he obliged. He was very deliberate and meticulous as he held my hand and spread it open so that he could elaborate on each line, and tell me what their meaning was. Then he looked up at me, and looked down at my hand again. He said, "Do you see this line here? I shook my head, yes. He said, "This is your life line, and from the looks of things, you will have a short life. Sometime between the ages of forty-two and forty-four, you will be in a terrible car accident, and that's going to take your life." I can't explain how I felt afterwards, but I wasn't fearful. I accredit that to thinking that I had at least twenty more years to live before I needed to be concerned. I got saved when I was thirty-seven years old. I was forty-seven when I had a flashback of the day that I had my palms read. I can only believe that God kept my mind clear of that memory until I was past the point where the enemy could use it to instill fear, which draws torment, and what is known as the law of attraction. A scripture comes to mind concerning fear. Job after having lost everything said..."The thing that I **greatly** feared has come upon me"...Job 3:25 (**KJV**) I used to be a worrywart, and even though I was now a Christian, I probably would have trembled with fear expecting to die every time I got into a car between the ages of forty-two and forty-four.

I made reference earlier to the care that we should take when listening to certain music and what we watch as a form of entertainment. Satan is the "prince of the power of the air", and he gains access through the things that we allow to seep in through the airwaves. They take up residence in our psyche and in our spirits where they begin to manifest in different ways to discomfiture our lives, our homes our families, our communities, and the list goes on. There have been times that while driving, a car would pass me or stop for a light beside me. The passengers are young children, the music is ridiculously loud, and the lyrics are blasting expletives. This is indicative of the atmosphere in the home. These innocent babies are being subjected to the lifestyles of adults who lack parental consciousness and self-control, and the effect is anything but positive. Their virgin ears and eyes are hearing and seeing things that are detrimental to their psyche. Like sponges they are soaking up things that they cannot properly process, but the evil one will do the processing for them. Our ears and eyes are gates. What are we opening our gates and the gates of our children to? Who are we giving access to? Television and the internet have become babysitters for many of our children. Gaming platforms are not moderated, and young children are exposed to such inappropriate language and material. Sex videos flood the internet, and some designers are targeting kids as young as seven years old. They are being demonically influenced by the programming and they need the protection and guidance of those who will navigate them through the subtle traps of deception set up by the enemy, whose end is always destruction.

"For all that is in the world - the lust of the flesh [craving for sensual gratification] the lust of the eyes [greedy longings of the mind], and the pride of life [assurance in one's own resources, or in the stability of earthly things] - these do not come from the Father but are of the world [itself]. And the world passes away, and disappears, and with it the forbidden cravings (the passionate desires, the lust) of it; but he who does the will of God and carries out His purposes in his life abides (remains) forever."

I Jo. 2:16-17 (AMPL)

We have given the enemy far too much access…far too much power! The world is expected to walk this way. They don't know any other way, but we as children of the Most High God must be accountable and steer clear of such carnal and careless behaviors. The Church has the power to right the wrongs that we see perpetuated in society today, but sadly stagnation, slumber, and an attitude of apathy is shamefully permeating the Church. It's as though we don't believe it is possible to utilize the authority that Jesus the Christ has given us to intervene and make the difference. The state of the Church today is alarming! We need a shaking and an awakening. The Church is in a lull.

God have mercy on us for being silent while hundreds of thousands of babies were being murdered across this nation every year, and billions of government dollars were awarded to those slaughterhouses while we accepted the lies of the deceiver that women were being cared for and given the utmost assistance. Yes…care for the women, but cease the massacre, and refrain from glorifying murder! We live in a culture of deception, and we are deceived if we think that there won't be a day of judgement. Nothing that we choose to do or not to do is without consequences.

The bible and prayer are taken out of schools while the series of the Harry Potter books, [which exalts witchcraft] are welcomed and made a part of the curriculum. In the process our children are being desensitized to the dangers of the occult. The correlation between the removal of the moral fiber and the decline of the public schools with the decision to cease all prayer and scripture reading, should be as clear as the nose on our faces. There are no government programs, no legislative action, no marching and demonstrations that can reverse the curse that has been given free reign in our society, and in the public education system. We see the increase in juvenile crime via school shootings, etc., illegal drug use, teachers being disrespected, assaulted, raped, robbed, and murdered. Remove the moral fiber, remove the power of God through prayer, and this is what we can expect. I get it that many parents have been derelict in their duties to train and discipline their children at home, however, the bible says that "one can put thousand to flight, two can put ten thousand to flight." If the prayers of the righteous avails much, then Christians should be able to pray and see results, regardless to what other religions are in the midst, and what they believe. We are still called the "**salt of the earth**, and **the light of the world**."

Are our schools employing witches and sorcerers? Have our schools become breeding grounds for witchcraft? These are fair questions, and should be considered. Let's face it… children are the perfect prey. Their innocence, their inquisitive, adventurous and naive natures all satiate the appetites of these perpetrators.

I was listening to a podcast in which a pastor was sharing how he went to pick his son up from school, and the teacher who greeted him was dressed in all black, and wore black lipstick and sported long black nails. Harry Potter books were on the desks, and the children were reading them. He approached the teacher, and told her that his child is a Christian, and does not read Harry Potter. She dismissed him by saying that they have a homework assignment from one of the books. The pastor refused to allow his son to participate, but stated that he would find an alternative. He later removed his child from the public school system.

Those who want to push this agenda will deny that any harm is being done, and instead will claim that It is only presented as a part of a fantasy world that all kids love. However, the language, activities, and symbolism all tell the real story.

We must deliberately keep our spiritual antennas tuned in and tuned up. Stay on the alert, because the second that we let our guard down and become so confident that all of our bases are covered, the adversary throws a dart. This is not a scare tactic. This is the word of God. The enemy is looking for those that are easy prey. They are sleep walking, they are preoccupied, they are distracted and intoxicated with the lusts of this world. These are the people of God, but they are not a threat to Satan's kingdom, instead they are the elect that offer no resistance to deception, but fall right into the deceiver's net.

Many times paths that lead to deception never even occur to us. Think about moving into a new home or apartment, and even moreso when you check into a hotel room. Walk through and pray. Plead the Blood of Jesus over every area and anoint every entry way of your dwelling place with oil. I remember when my son and daughter-in-law first found their dream home in the Elkins Park area of Philly. We were talking on the phone one night, and Derek told me that the former owners had gone through a bitter divorce, and that he had found symbols painted outside in the pool area, in the basement, and around the walls outside of the basketball court. I immediately told him that we need to pray and bind the powers of darkness over, in and around the home. We also took authority over and bound the spirit of divorcement and all residue associated with it. And of course we appropriated the Blood of Jesus.

There are so many things that we bring into our home that can attract demonic activity and give spirits legal rights to defile our dwellings and harass us. Some things are a welcome mat that communicate to the unseen demon world that they have our permission to co-habit. Deception creeps in through shiny objects; the dream catchers, crystals, masks, statues, artifacts, 5-pointed pentagrams, emblems of various lodges, such as signets and seals that mark Greek fraternities and sororities, and busts and statues of other deities whose history and origins are of an occult or demonic nature.

Let's talk about crystals, which are a beautiful and striking creation of God's handi-work. I just want to clarify that crystals in and of themselves are like money...neutral.

We use crystal in a myriad of ways; in decorating our homes, as jewelry and decorative art, etc., however, just as perversion is so prevalent in God's intended purpose for other things, so it is for the use of crystals. For centuries crystals have been used in idol worship to ward off evil spirits, to emanate good vibrations, attract health, wealth, and romance, to draw good and protective spirits, to cast a spell, perform rituals, and to absorb bad energy. And don't forget the crystal ball for fortune telling. They are also used in the practice of crystal healing, a pseudoscience that claims to heal various ailments by carefully placing them on the body to line up with the chakras (the psychic energy centers). None of these superstitious beliefs are biblical. In fact they are idol practices. For our own protection the word of God warns us against connecting to or engaging in anything relating to superstition or the occult.

There shall not be found among you anyone who makes his son or his daughter pass through the fire, or one who practices witchcraft, or a soothsayer (those who claim to forsee the future), or one who interprets omens, or a sorcerer, or one who conjures spells, or a medium or a spiritist, or one who calls up the dead. For all who do these things are an abomination to the Lord, and because of these

abominations the Lord your God drives them out from before you. Deuteronomy. 18:10-12 (NKJV)

These things are anti-Christ, ungodly, idolatrous and an abomination to the Lord because they are looked to as a source to replace God Himself. He alone is our source; our provider, protector, healer, and our well of plenty. Things that are conjured up to manipulate the spirit world is categorized as witchcraft. It is still a form of idol worship, and is no different than engaging the stars, moon, or the sun to draw from them the things that only our God can provide. God warned Moses in **Deuteronomy 4:19** with these words....

"And take heed, lest you lift your eyes to heaven, and when you see the sun, the moon, and the stars, all the hosts of heaven, you feel driven to worship them and serve them..."

Concerning the Prophetic

Be cautious in chasing the gifts. There are some who run to every meeting categorized as "prophetic" looking for a word, and the spirit of deception lurks nearby ready to accommodate. Some dial in to prophetic hot lines, which are only glorified psychic hot lines, and are just as plentiful. One can simply go online and make requests for free personal prophecy. Headlines will read..."Get your prophetic word today. God wants to speak to you!" Believers who run to and fro looking for guidance from a source aside from Holy Spirit to lead and guide their lives are opening the door for the counterfeit to come in and it could be catastrophic. Our omniscient Father knew there would be such, and again He gives us a warning that is over two-thousand years old.

For false christs and false prophets will rise and show great signs and wonders to deceive if possible, even the elect....

Matthew 24:24 (NKJV)

God used old testament prophets to foretell the future; to warn, to rebuke, to give revelation, guidance, and to counsel His people as necessary. Under the new dispensation, prophets are not set in the church to guide the lives of God's people, but prophecy should edify, exhort and comfort the Believer. If you get a personal word from one who proclaims to be a prophet, it should bear witness with your spirit to confirm that which God has already spoken to you. A prophet is not a fortune teller. We are to rely on God's word, and the leading of Holy Spirit; the inward witness, not by seeking a word from someone.

"Beloved, do not believe every spirit, but test the spirits whether they are of God; because many false prophets have gone out into the world." ...

I John 4:1 (NKJV).

The gifts of the Spirit do not operate in the flesh. According to *I Corinthians 12:11*, the gift of prophesy is governed by none other than Holy Spirit and is given as He wills to an individual to declare revelation from God, who always used prophets to reveal truth to His people; a truth that can only be discerned by God speaking through a person.

The bible tells us not to despise prophecy... **Thessalonians. 5:20-21**

We cannot afford to discount what Jesus has set in the church for our benefit (*Ephesians 4:12*), because of the operation of the counterfeit, but by the same token we are not to believe everything that is spoken to us with the label of "prophesy" attached to it. Remember that the words of a true prophet will be fulfilled.

I was invited to a luncheon and "prophetic" meeting by a friend in ministry, and I reluctantly agreed to go. After lunch was over the prophetess got up and began her sermon. After ten minutes or so she began to work the room, going to different people with a personal word of prophecy, which seemed to be mostly vague generalities with only a few exceptions. As she moved on with her message she was eloquent in speech, and really began to stir the people up. Then she asked how many needed a financial breakthrough. Well, that question appealed to most everyone present. Then she hit them with a scripture, and for the sake of demonstration I will use Isaiah 1:19. She told the people that Isaiah 1:19 says, **"That if you are willing and obedient, you will eat the good of the land."** I need 100 people to give $119. today. If you are ready to get your breakthrough, stand to your feet! People stood all over the room. She continued, "I need you to form two lines. Those who will give $119.00, line up to my right, and those who will give any amount, stand to my left. My spirit grumbled within me. The people went forward and formed their respective lines. She gave each of them a word as they left their gifts at the alter. I was seated at one of the tables in the front, but I did not budge, nor did I feel led to, nor did I feel any conviction at all. These are the kinds of things that are done in the name of the Lord, but in reality it is all for self gratification, the need to be popular and admired by people, and financial gain.

God made this statement in Jeremiah. 14:14 (NKJV)

"The prophets prophesy lies in my name. I have not sent them, commanded them, nor spoken to them; they prophesy to you a false vision, divination, a worthless thing, and the deceit of their heart."

This person was able to pull off a few more of these meetings, but people began to catch on, and after awhile the attendance dwindled to nothing.

This does not fall far from what we called scams. Scams are just another word for deception. No matter the category of the scam, within it is a plot, a plan, a scheme someone has been deceived. Someone has been lied to, cheated, manipulated, taken advantage of, or swindled. Any way you cut it and whatever label you give it….it is still **deception**.

As I conclude, I cannot take credit for following message from a blog that I scrolled upon, and saw as a **"Must share."**

Satan in a fanciful vignette summonsed three of his demons and gave them an assignment.

He commanded, "You are to go throughout the earth, and I want you to deceive as many people as you possible can, causing them to be lost. But before you go I want to hear how you plan to deceive them.

The first demon stepped forward and said, I'm going to tell all these people that there is no God. Satan shook his head, saying, "That would work only on a few but most people wouldn't buy it. There's too much evidence that a Creator God exists. I reject your plan, because it wouldn't deceive enough people.

The second demon came before him and said confidently, "I will teach everybody that there is no hell." Satan let out a roaring laugh. "People know better than that. They know there is a place where unrepentant sinners go and burn, never to live again. Your plan would never work either. It may deceive a few people, but eventually they would catch on to you."

The third demon rose and said, "I will tell them that there's no need to hurry."

Satan said, "Go! You will deceive everybody." Revelation 12:9

My fervent prayer is: "Father, open our spiritual eyes, and. I forgive those who have trespassed against me and I release them to You. Show me the areas of my life that do not please you. I need Your skillful and Godly wisdom to permeate every area of my life today. It is my desire to walk circumspect before You all the days of my life and to be that part of the Body without spot or wrinkle or blemish or any such thing. I thank You that You create in me a clean heart and renew a right spirit within me. I thank you for clean hands and a pure heart. I thank You for the mind of Christ and that Christ be formed in me daily. I put off the old man and I put on the Lord Jesus Christ and make no provisions for the flesh. Father I thank You that I am free from every evil spirit that would try to rule over my life. I decree that only Your Spirit, True and Living God, will rule and reign over my life, over my family, over my household, and over the ministry that You have entrusted to me..

Purge me, prune me, mold me, shape me into that which You may use for Your pleasure and Your glory. Gut me out Lord, so that I am emptied of anything that does not resemble You. Help me to know Your purpose for my life that I may be all that You have called me to be. I purpose not to leave any door open for the enemy's access. I thank You for keen discernment as Your Counsel speaks to me. I increase in Your knowledge and I am extremely sensitive to Your Holy Spirit. I surrender my all to You in the matchless Name and by the precious Blood of Yeshua.... Amen

The bible does say that we are to thank God in all things. I thank God in the things that I have come through, because I have been given a perspective on life that I otherwise would not have had. Because of the experiences that I have been able to share, someone will be the better, just as I am. When we are going "through", the flesh is rebelling and it doesn't feel good. Yet, I believe that all tests and trials are a part of the process that sharpens and strengthens us so that we become an asset to the Body of Christ and not a hindrance. My mentor would say. "There is no testimony without the test."

Just as gold goes through the fire and is purified and refined, so are we when we take these tests and pass them...coming out on the other side fit for the Master's use.

"For false christs and false prophets will rise and show great signs and wonders to deceive, if possible, even the elect." Mat. 24:24 (NKJV)

About the Author

Nanci C. Nixon is a licensed and ordained minister of the gospel of Jesus Christ. She is a graduate of Temple University, where she received her Bachelor of Arts degree in Communications & Theatre. After many years of being a resident actress and Annual Fund Coordinator for Freedom Theater in her native hometown of Philadelphia, PA she was invited to Los Angeles after being cast in a stage production as the leading lady. She would eventually make Los Angeles her home and planned to continue pursuing her acting career while working as a counselor/case manager for the Los Angeles Community Mental Health Department.

Her plans drastically shifted after surrendering her life to Jesus Christ in a Sunday morning worship service. Just prior to retiring, she answered the call on her life and began her journey into ministry after serving over a decade as a personal ministries counselor at her home church.

Called in the office of Teacher, Minister Nanci Nixon is a graduate of Crenshaw Christian Center's Ministry Training Institute in Los Angeles, CA and is a recipient of their Faculty Award for Excellence in Commitment and Leadership. Upon completing her studies she was indoctrinated into the Immediate Pastoral Support unit of the Ministerial Assistance Program where her service ranged from Teacher's assistant and prayer counselor, to teaching Discipleship and Fundamental classes.

Minister Nixon has served as board member and Secretary of the Board of Directors for **Hosanna Broadcasting Network… "The Voice of Jesus Christ"** in Long Beach, CA. for the past five years. She is a former board member of Transformed By the Word Ministries in Scotts Hill, NC, and formerly served on the Elder board at Livingstone's Tabernacle in Hampstead, NC where she taught weekly bible studies with a strong focus on her passion....**The Person of Holy Spirit; His Purpose, His Gifts, The Power, The Benefits, The Evidence.** While serving as an elder she also incorporated Personal Ministries counseling classes and training as a part of the Ministry of Helps.

In "**Can the Elect Be Deceived**"Minister Nixon candidly shares her personal stories of deception. Her book is currently in the process of being written into a screen play.

She is founder of **J.O.I.W.O.O. Ministries** (pronounced Joy-Woo) Acronym for **"Jesus On The Inside, Working On The Outside"**

A part of this works mission is to target and teach young women to exemplify Christ through their lifestyles, being earthly examples who endeavor to walk circumspect before Him, living a life above reproach.

Minister Nixon has taught women's bible study at Crenshaw Christian Center, Los Angeles, and has taught a weekly bible study at Dare U 2 Care Transitional Living Center for over a decade.

She has received an Honorary Doctorate of Divinity Degree from St. Thomas Christian University , Jacksonville, FL.

Printed by Libri Plureos GmbH in Hamburg, Germany